I0822167

Stars Calling

The Legend of Ghaleon Series

By Theresa Biehle

BOOK 1: SPIRITS ENTWINED

BOOK 2: STARS CALLING

Stars Calling

Book 2 of the Legend of Ghaleon

Theresa Biehle

This is a work of fiction. All of the characters, organizations, and events portrayed in this novel are either products of the author's imagination or are used fictitiously.

First Edition

ISBN: 979-8-9857388-2-7

Edited by Theresa Biehle

Artwork by Theresa Biehle

www.theresabiehle.com

Acknowledgments

A special thank you to my Alpha readers including my Mum, Andrew Biehle, and Alex Williams for their valuable feedback. Also, many thanks to all my family and friends who gave me feedback on my artwork as it evolved.

Previous Character and Location Glossary

Characters

Kylie (Kye-lee):

Long wavy blonde hair. Green eyes. Spirit color is green. Started the first book at age 19. Princess of Arbore. Utilized by Saliek as decoy Spirit Master to protect Mory. In love with Mory. Bonded to pegasus Starshine.

Mory (Mo-ree):

Shaggy blonde hair. Blue eyes. Spirit color is purple. Started the first book at age 19. In love with Kylie. Spirit Master. Has Ghaleon's artifacts: Sword, Shield, Cloak.

Anik (An-nick):

Slightly curly, unruly auburn hair. Brown eyes. Spirit color is orange. Started the first book at age 21. Junior member of the Saliek. Specializes in elemental control. Bonded to pegasus Bandit.

Zhannah (Zan-nah):

Blonde hair characteristically braided back for battles. Spirit color is yellow. Member of the Saliek. Raised Kylie with Regithal while on Thaer. Dual wields swords. Bonded to pegasus Storm.

Regithal (Reg-i-thal):

Very tall with broad shoulders. Dark hair that falls to shoulders. Ice blue eyes. Spirit color sky blue. He is the Saliek'an (leader of the Saliek). Intimidating person with a jovial personality. Raised Kylie with Zhannah while on Thaer. Wields a large great sword. Bonded to pegasus Valor.

Scilla (Sil-lah):

Short dark hair. Pale lavender eyes. Pale white skin that is very sensitive to light. Member of the Saliek. Home planet is Tendyis. Raised Mory on Thaer in the Ancient Archives. Used to be able to see the future. Lost ability in the first book suddenly. Kaitzen's twin sister.

Dainn (Dane):

Shaved head. Dark brown eyes. Covered in Ignet tattoos. Extremely strong. Battles with fists. Koth magic. Dark caramel skin. Bound to his duty to protect Elasche.

Elasche (Ee-lash):

Long, nearly black hair. Caramel skin. Healer. Spirit color is black. Princess of Mahashta. Held hostage by Sonu as his betrothed in the first book until escaped with Kylie and Anik's help.

Telovi (Tel-o-vee) a.k.a. Vi (Vee):

Perfectly proportioned miniature human fairy. No larger than the size of a hand. Light purple skin. Dark purple hair. Her transparent wings flit so quickly when hovering that you can barely see them move. Very energetic. Started traveling with Mory after he visited the invisible fairy oasis near Mahashta in the first book. Has mirage magic which can make things hidden.

Sonu (So-new):

Blonde hair. Green eyes. Kylie's brother. Antagonist in the first book who was being controlled by Kaitzen. Prior to partial death, he was the Prince of Arbore. Currently, being held in between life and death until he redeems himself by helping the universe defeat Kaitzen.

Kaitzen (Kate-zen) a.k.a. Zen (Zen):

Long black hair. Pale white skin that is sensitive to light. Antagonist in the first book. Scilla's twin brother. Home planet is Tendyis. Controls creatures on Krael by trading knowledge of their future. Fled Krael through the portal to Tendyis at the end of the first book.

Locations

Thaer (Thay-er):

Place where Spirit magic does not work. Scilla, Zhannah, and Regithal raised Kylie and Mory there near the dormant volcano, Mount Liriken. Ancient Archives are located here. Colors here are dull in comparison to Krael.

Krael (Kray-el):

Planet where Spirit magic is prevalent. Very colorful. Cities of Arbore and Mahashta are located here. Saliek's main forces are here. Ignet reside here.

Blaet (Blay-et):

Planet in the same solar system as Krael and Thaer with no Spirit magic.

Tendyis (Ten-dye-is):

Planet in a different solar system where seer magic is prevalent.

KRAEL
FROSTLANDS
GOLDEN PLAINS
ARBORE
SALIEK
SENTINEL MOUNTAINS
VAST AMOUNTS OF OCEAN
DIADUST DESERT
IGNET
MAHASHTA
FAIRY OASIS
MAP NOT TO SCALE

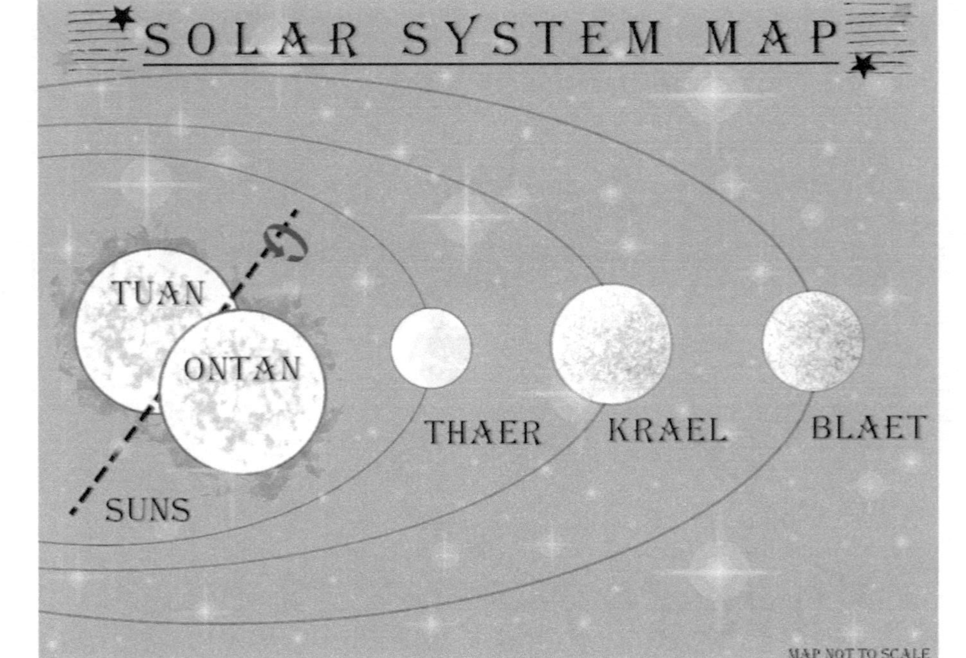
SOLAR SYSTEM MAP
TUAN
ONTAN
SUNS
THAER
KRAEL
BLAET
MAP NOT TO SCALE

Prologue

Many years before on the planet of eternal twilight: Tendyis.

The pale light of day on Tendyis was waning into the deep darkness of night as the white light of Larian sank below the horizon in a purple haze. The dimmer yellow glow of the stars was left to light the cool, dreary night, peering through patches of grey clouds. A slight drizzle wet the thick green-blue grass that blanketed the ground around a small, isolated town. The houses were spread far enough apart to give each family their privacy but close enough together where you could distinguish your neighbors. Inside the windows of the houses, the dim glow of aromatic candles indicated the presence of occupants inside. The usual clattering of conversations and evening meals was going on within the majority of the houses, and the hum could be heard in the quiet outside if one were to listen carefully.

Inside a particular house, with a tire swing hanging from a gnarled tree out front, a young girl sat on the landing of the stairs to the second floor, legs swinging over the last stair. Her hands were cupped about her face and propped up by her elbows on her knobby knees bared by her long nightshirt. Her mother had put her and her brother to bed early that night, but she was not tired yet, and her curiosity had always been piqued when she was turned away from something. Kaitzen was content to stay in his room and work on his latest scheme.

Her parents had forbidden them both from using their natural-born talents as seers, a talent that was shared by the majority of Tendyians, because of the complications that arose from it. They believed in living a simpler life here in a small town without everyone meddling in what was to come. Whatever would be, would be, and they would reap the benefits or weather the storm as needed. The residents of the small town that surrounded them all maintained a similar mindset and lived in some sort of secluded harmony from the rest of their planet. Kaitzen was none too happy about this decision and secretly did experiments in his bedroom, planning to escape this life once he came of age. Scilla, his twin sister, was the only one aware of these experiments. She was willing to keep her brother's secret, as they were the closest of friends, and she hadn't personally seen him do anything too worrisome yet.

Her father had come home in one of his moods and had gone to the cupboard where they kept the lakka root concentrate again. Scilla was used to the yelling now. It had been happening more frequently lately. One time she had even come downstairs to try to reason with them, but that had gotten her into even more trouble, and was not appreciated by either of her parents. This time was one of the scary times. One of the times when she would not go downstairs, no matter how much her curiosity prodded her, and she would watch silently from her darkened perch. She was sadly sure that when she awoke tomorrow her mother would bear some sort of black and blue mark that she would deftly cover with her makeup, or she would wear a long-sleeved shirt when the weather would deem something lighter more appropriate. She could hear crashing in the kitchen as her father screamed obscenities at her mother. She never did understand why he needed the lakka root so frequently, and her mother tried to keep him away from it.

The crashing was getting louder this time, and she saw her mother running for the stairs, calling Scilla and Kaitzen's names. Her cream dress that she wore that day was rumpled and torn at one of the sleeves. Her dark hair, matching the color of Scilla's, flew out behind her. Kaitzen came running out of his room, hearing the fear and urgency in his mother's voice, and passed Scilla as he ran down the stairs. Scilla, always the more hesitant of the two, hung there for a moment meeting the desperate dark eyes of her mother as she feverishly waved her down off of her perch.

Then, as Scilla was about to come down, she saw him behind her. The man who was supposed to be her father. Dark fire glowed in his eyes as he carried the remnants of what used to be the cabinet that held the drinks that he deeply desired. His body, toned from years of physical labor in his woodworking shop, wielded a splintered wood plank as a weapon. Scilla tried in vain to tell her mother to leave, to escape through the front door that was feet away, but it was too little too late. Her screams and flailing arms were not enough. The crazed man let the board fly, and he hit his mark. The cream dress slowly turned red as the life fizzled out in her mother's eyes, and she sunk slowly to the floor.

Scilla shrieked. Kaitzen ran. The running boy caught the attention of the monster. Scilla flew from her perch to her mother's side frantically trying to figure out what to do. She desperately reached for her forbidden magic, something she hadn't done in years, in order to see if there was anything she could do. It was too late. All paths in this instance led to her mother's death. So, she held her mother in her spindly child's arms the best that she could as her mother whispered nonsensical words to no one in particular. Scilla called upon all her strength, inner and physical, as she held her mother tight. She told her words of comfort in her pain as she simultaneously cried, not knowing what else to do. When her mother's pain was gone and there was no more breath within her body, Scilla turned her attention back to her house.

Her father was kicking and beating Kaitzen with the same wooden plank. With the loss of her mother so fresh a wound on her small heart, the blood still fresh on her hands and clothes, she was not about to let the monster take her best friend and brother as well. She would protect him and not let this beast harm anyone else. She looked around and found miniature toy logs that were strewn across the floor. She and Kaitzen had been building houses with them earlier that day. She picked them up and one by one hurled them at the monster that had once been her father. A person who had once carried her on his shoulders as she giggled and had pushed her on the tire swing out front before walking her to school. The person who had lovingly built the many wooden toys that she played with regularly around the house. The person who used to tell her bedtime stories and play silly games with her. The betrayal of her implicit trust and respect for this man is what hurt her the most. "Pick on someone your own size, you brute!" she screamed with all the intensity of the fear, anger, and disgust she could muster in her broken soul. After a few well-aimed throws, she managed to draw his attention away from Kaitzen, who was now a crumpled mess in the corner.

The raging monster roared and then directed his anger at her. She had nowhere to go in the short distance that he stood away from her. Not even the front door was close enough for her small body to reach and open before he could take the three big steps across the living room to her. Before she knew what had happened, she was in his grasp. His strong hand tightened its grip around her small neck as he lifted her and held her against the wall at arm's length. Her legs dangled helplessly in midair.

In the corner of her eye, she saw Kaitzen drag himself out the front door. Good, he was safe. Relief flooded through her momentarily. The monster gripped her tighter, and the pain of her crushing esophagus ran through her. She began to feel her lower body numbing, and the lack of oxygen began to burn. She realized now what she had done. She had sacrificed herself for her brother. He had run, but he was safe now. As she struggled with the pain, Scilla eventually decided that she was not going to die with her eyes closed.

She was going to face this monster eye to eye, so he could watch the life leave her body, just as she had seen her mother's spark take leave. The life of the child he was supposed to love and care for. Defiantly, she opened her tear-stained eyes and peered into those of the monster. What she saw there terrified her even more; the hatred, the anger, the disappointment, all in the eyes of someone who was supposed to love her. He was supposed to care for her. He didn't. She held the stare until her head was too light for her to create a lucid thought.

For a moment, she thought that she saw something in her attacker's eyes. A change, a hint of recognition, or even remorse. His grip slackened around her neck, and he threw her onto the couch nearby. He said something to her, but she couldn't make it out through the drums sounding in her head. The return of oxygen to her limbs hurt worse than it being taken away, and she fell into a deep sleep.

***

Kaitzen ran. His little legs churned beneath him as reflexively as his heartbeat. His mind whisked between thoughts, fueled by the blinding fear that presently overpowered his mind. He ran into the streets, feeling the gravel poke the soles of his bare feet and the aching pain in his back from the board with which he had been beaten. The people in the houses nearby noticed his flight, but ignored it, going back to their dinners and evening past times. They all whispered of his father's problem behind closed doors, but no one ever wanted to get involved. They used the excuse of it not being polite to pry into other people's business, but the truth was they were too lazy to care. They were too lazy to stand up for someone when they would have to risk their own necks or reputation in the process. It was easier to accept the status quo, pretend like everything was okay as is, and let life happen to them. They would let others make the decisions in their lives for them, then they would never have to feel accountable for anything bad that ever came of their decisions. They would always have someone else to blame and point their fingers at. It was easier to judge others for their faulty decisions and look back on the situation saying what should have been done, rather than to be the one to take action.

Kaitzen hated them. All of them. The hatred roared through his veins with an intensity akin to burning. Banish them all to the unknown depths of the universe. They all treated his family as some sort of taboo, and none of the other children were allowed to play with him or his sister. They all hid in the safety and supposed ignorance of their day-to-day lives. He would leave this place. He wanted to leave it now. The clouds opened up pouring sheets of rain onto Kaitzen. Something nagged at the back of his mind… A cold raindrop hit him in his eye, causing him to shake his head, and the thought came to him as the motion tumbled his thoughts. Scilla was still back there. The cool rain felt nearly freezing for a moment as the recent memory came back to him, as well as the realization that she was in grave danger after her little stunt to rescue him from his father's wrath.

With a groan that was silenced by a boom of thunder, Kaitzen halted his retreat. Mud from the gravel road splattered all over him as he hastily reversed his direction. With a second wind of breath, he ran back the way he had come from with the lights of the nearby houses blurring as he galloped past them. He tried to grasp for his seering talent and attempted delving into the immediate future to see if Scilla's life was stable or hinging on the action of someone… namely himself. He did not have control of his mind now though because his emotions were too strong, and the visions that had assaulted him randomly before had never given him a glimpse into this future, at least not that he could remember or discern the meaning of. So, on he ran in the pouring rain back to his house. His feet would slide randomly in the mud at times, but he only fell once skinning his knee and palms on the rough stones in the road.

When he returned to the front door of his house, he paused for a moment. He knew that his mother's body would be lying lifeless on the floor when he entered. He had to mentally prepare himself for that. He listened closely for any noises that would indicate what had transpired inside. There were none. At least none that he could hear over the storm swirling around him. He felt the intensity of the burn of his hatred increase. It was mixed with fear and anger now as well. His skin felt visibly warm in the cool rain, and his head began to feel as though it would explode from the pressure building up within. When he couldn't take it anymore, he burst through the front door.

He scanned the horrible scene, looking beyond his mother's body to see his sister lying unmoving on the couch covered in blood and tears. His father knelt before her with his forehead on the cushion and hand outstretched toward her. In his blinding rage, Kaitzen ran into the kitchen, grabbed a cooking knife in each hand, and ran at the stationary man. "Die Monster!" He screamed and forced both the knives into his father's back where each shoulder met his neck. His father screamed a last painful screech before falling backward, pushing the knives further into his body.

Kaitzen felt the enmity leak away for a moment as he looked down into his father's eyes… they were no longer those of a monster as they shone crystal blue and empty at the ceiling. He looked up and saw his reflection in a window, now the monstrous, blood-shot, rage-filled eyes belonged to him. He clawed helplessly at his face. What had he done?! He looked back to the couch in confusion. The tears on his sister's body had been his father's, and before he had fallen back onto the floor, he had been holding Scilla's limp hand in his own. Before the flood of memories of his father could penetrate his mind, he threw up mental walls to block them.

Refusing to think anymore, he crawled onto the couch next to his sister, curled into a ball next to her, and fell into a nightmare-riddled sleep for the remainder of the night.

***

The next afternoon they came, when the kids didn't show up at school, nor the parents at work. The carnage they saw was absolute, and the smell of rot had begun to fill the air as the survivors curled close and bloody on the couch. Clearly, they were the ones guilty of this monstrosity. Someone had to be, or else the town's people would have to feel guilty for their inaction. "To the portals with them!" The chant was taken up by those of the town, and the two children were taken by the local authorities to be tried and sentenced at the Plain of Portals.

Chapter 1

The trees blushed as the sweet breath of autumn swept by, touching them with her golden kiss as she passed. Scilla followed her in the chill of the evening down a trail near the Saliek camp while on her nightly walk, slowly drifting away into her thoughts. The vibrant trees that surrounded her had taken years to grow as tall and magnificent as they were. With age they strengthened, making it easier for them to weather the storms and withstand the beating of time. Scilla admired their beauty and strength as her mind turned over recent events, readying herself for what she must do next.

It had been over a year since she had last seen Kaitzen in a vision leaving Krael via the portal in the mountains that they were exiled here by so many years ago. It was a risky move on his part, driven by desperation. Both their powers of foresight had abruptly ceased on Krael, and she knew how much Kaitzen had relied upon and revered his power. She had no idea if he was still alive, but if he was, she had a good idea of where he had gone. He must have come to the same conclusion that she had. If he returned to his home planet of Tendyis, his powers might return to him. Mory, the Spirit Master, had the only traveling cloak known to unerringly transport its wearer to a planet that far away safely. There was no small chance that Kaitzen was floating lifelessly somewhere in the space between Krael and Tendyis.

Unfortunately, the chance that he was alive was large enough to have Scilla worried, as he had managed to steal a Saliek cloak before he left. Saliek cloaks could ensure successful travel for short distances across space and increase your chances of survival to further away locations. Kaitzen had worked Krael into a nice little mess while he used his power of foresight to manipulate not only the people of Krael, but also the creatures and demons that occupied it. Knowledge of the future was a powerful bargaining chip that he used very well. Scilla could not let him come back here and ruin all the reparations that they had made, and she found her conscience constantly nagging at her that he could be doing the same somewhere else. She felt that it was her duty to stop him.

She had waited this long year in order to give Mory enough time to rebuild the city of Arbore and help bring peace back to Krael, as was his duty as the Spirit Master. She had felt a small hope that Kaitzen may return on his own in the meantime, though she had no such luck. Mory had acquired all three pieces of Ghaleon's equipment the previous year. This proved that he was indeed the Spirit Master of this age and ensured that he was destined for more than the usual Spirit Master. He was currently residing in Arbore with the decoy Spirit Master that became Mory's beloved, Kylie.

Kylie had met her birth parents for the first time since she was a baby and had accepted them into a part of her life. The role of mother and father to her had been played by Regithal and Zhannah of the Saliek until she had turned 19. It turned out that her heart was large enough for all of them to reside within it. Her blood parents had recently been trying to teach her how to fulfill her role as the princess of Arbore, as her elder brother Sonu had presumably perished in his search for the cloak of Ghaleon. Kylie was not taking to the experience very well. Social etiquette and politics were not her strong points. Elasche, the princess of Mahashta, returned to Arbore occasionally to provide what aid she could as a friend to Kylie.

After Mory had acquired Ghaleon's cloak, Dainn and Elasche had returned to Mahashta where Elasche had a dramatic falling out with her parents for forcing her to marry a psychopath like Prince Sonu just to expand their country's influence, and she began her study with the Ignet elders. She never wanted to be unable to defend herself again. Her weapon of choice had been the staff, and she was learning extremely quickly. She was a late starter for those of the Ignet and one of the very few women. Elasche had expressed her concerns over the whispering and standoffish nature of the other Ignet toward her but never took it to heart. Never before had one of the royal family of Mahashta decided to pursue the path of the Ignet, so they couldn't be blamed for their mutterings. Dainn was ever by her side as he always had been.

Anik, who had expressed what could only be described as puppy love toward Elasche, had returned with Regithal and Zhannah to the Saliek camp in the Sentinel mountains surrounding Arbore. They visited each other on occasion but were now on more friendly than romantic terms with Elasche's pursuits within the Ignet and his own training and studying within the Saliek. Regithal, Zhannah, and Anik had been primarily occupied with helping Mory grow as the Spirit Master to become more proficient and comfortable with his powers as well as sword technique.

Certain members of the Saliek endeavored to identify Kaitzen's informant, whom they suspected had infiltrated the Saliek camp or was lurking near enough to spy. They had yet to locate this informant and were beginning to think that they had retired when Kaitzen left, or were lying dormant, awaiting their next opportunity. Scilla had tried to convince people that Kaitzen's ability to see the future could have been all that he needed to decipher Kylie's whereabouts, but natives of Krael were not used to having seers around, so they wasted time and effort searching for an informant that likely did not exist.

The Saliek, as a whole, had accompanied Mory across Krael attempting to set right what Kaitzen had disturbed.

Everything was in a significantly more stable state now. Enough time had passed. It was time for Scilla to take action against Kaitzen.

The brittle leaves that had already fallen and blanketed the ground, crunched beneath her black boots and skirt as she altered her path to stop by Regithal's tents. He was the commander of the Saliek, the Saliek'an, and she trusted his opinion on important matters such as this one. As she exited the forest paths and neared the lines of Saliek tents, a rainbow of colorful pairs of eyes turned in her direction and peered at her curiously from under their drawn black hoods as they traversed the orderly aisles of tents. Very few knew of her descendance from another planet, one of eternal twilight, that had colored her skin the palest of hues and made it difficult for her to withstand the bright daylight of Krael. She had become known as the "Night Walker" or the "Lady of Shadows" behind closed doors.

She stopped outside Regithal's tents and called in to him to announce her presence before entering. He invited her to come inside, so she smoothly slid her slender body in between the heavy, thick, fabric entrance flaps. A fire crackled warmly in the corner surrounded by stones that directed the smoke out of the tent. The Saliek tents had been in the Sentinels long enough that they had become semi-permanent structures. Breaking down the camp would be a non-trivial task if it was ever required. Regithal was sitting at a desk staring down at a pile of papers with his glowing blue eyes, his straight black hair falling slightly over his face. "You know, Scilla, feeding an army is not nearly as exciting as leading one into battle," Regithal said with a slight smirk on his face before pushing the pile of papers away from his view and turning his attention to her. "What brings you here tonight?"

Scilla's pale lavender eyes met Regithal's bright blue ones, and she stated gravely, "I think the time has come that I return to Tendyis, Regithal. The watching devices that the

Saliek constructed around the portal Kaitzen escaped through have not indicated that he, or anyone, has arrived through it for the past year. We have cleaned up most of the mess that he made on Krael, and just his absence has righted many issues, leaving his minions with no one to turn to and direct them. Yet, I am afraid that his absence here implies his presence in another world where he is wreaking havoc that needs to be contained."

Regithal leaned back in his wooden chair, placed his hands on his head, and looked to the ceiling, humming. "I do not doubt your assessment, Scilla. Mory has indeed grown in this past year and has come into his abilities naturally and skillfully. I suppose you would require his assistance, as he owns Ghaleon's cloak. It would not be in our best interest to let someone like you perish. Moreover, I know he is destined for far more than the settling of conflict on this planet."

Scilla nodded and added, "I also think Kylie would be a good asset to our party. She is clearly unhappy in her role as princess of Arbore, and to be honest, her talents are being wasted on politics and social gatherings. Maybe she can retire into that position after we've saved a few worlds from certain destruction."

Regithal chuckled heartily at the mention of the girl he had raised as a daughter for years, "Yes, I do wholeheartedly agree with that! I sure would love to see her smile again. She is so overly stressed dealing with high society and other people's perceptions of her. She was raised in a small town where she knew everyone, throwing knives at practice targets. Expecting her to gracefully put down her knives and instead handle hundreds of strangers daily is a bit of a stretch. Nowadays, only the presence of Mory can bring a smile to her lips and a giggle to her voice. Additionally, I would be interested to see if our mind link worked as far away as Tendyis, and we could keep informed through our connection."

Scilla was quite content with how this conversation was going, “I am so very glad that we are on the same wavelength, Regithal. If it’s okay with you, I’d like to start preparing tomorrow.”

“Your request is granted, Scilla. Best of luck on your mission. Please take good care of Kylie for me. I know she would tell me that she can take care of herself, but knowing you’ll have your eyes watching over her would greatly ease my worries,” Regithal replied with a touch of uneasiness in his voice.

Scilla smiled reassuringly, “I’ve kept an eye on her for years on Thaer. It would be difficult to break myself of the habit now, Regithal. Worry not! I will keep my eyes on her for you.”

“Thank you, Scilla, you have my sincerest thanks.” Regithal removed his hands from his head and put them back on the desk where he began to fiddle with a pen that was sitting there. The focus in his eyes drifted away momentarily, “I think I will check on Kylie tonight and tell her the good news myself. I believe there is some party going on in Arbore that she was supposed to attend. This should make the night more bearable for her.” Regithal chuckled again, “Wasn’t it you who always nagged her about wearing dresses on Thaer?”

“All a part of my act, Regithal. You knew that.”

“Yes, but it still greatly amuses me to tell you that she has been wearing dresses to parties for the past year, tucking her knives away within the folds of the fabric. This has gotten her into a bit of a situation at times.” Regithal deftly handled the pen as though it was a knife and made a quick motion to set it horizontally across the neck of an unexpecting soldier figurine on his desk. “If you get my meaning.” Regithal returned the death-wielding pen to his desk, laughing heartily in his amusement at his daughter’s inability to fit in with high society.

Scilla shook her head with a smile tickling the edges of her lips, "That does not surprise me at all, Regithal. Oh, how I wish I could have been there to see the look on that poor soul's face."

"No one messes with my Kylie!" Regithal said proudly before dismissing Scilla for the evening.

Scilla returned to her walk within the darkened forest to sort through her thoughts on what needed to be accomplished before she would leave for Tendyis. A sharp pang resonated through her stomach. She would be going home for the first time in hundreds of years, without her power of foresight. It would be possible that everyone else there could see the future, except her. That prospect scared her. She would be at the mercy of the masses, a tool to be used by whoever realized it first. She would have to be very careful. With any luck, she would have her power back the moment she set foot on Tendyis, but there were no guarantees.

She had learned to get by on Krael with just her Spirit during this past year, but it was like someone had taken her security blanket away. The talent that was hers alone –and Kaitzen's, but she hadn't realized that until later– had disappeared. She had no idea why or how, but she could no longer see the paths of the future. Scilla had foreseen this event, but the shock of actually living with it had been a hard concept to swallow. She had done sufficiently on Krael, but this was a world where no one else could see the future. On Tendyis, it was the exact opposite. The light within her heart, Andolin, would have encouraged her to go, regardless of her fear or if she could see the future or not. He would be there with her always and help to guide her through.

***

A crystal chandelier twinkled in the dim lights of the dance hall of Arbore castle, dotting the navy carpets with white sparkles that made it seem as though one was walking amidst the stars in a clear night sky. Silver and gold garland intertwined and swirled high above the congregation while navy blue origami stars floated around its shimmering waves. The bride and groom were sharing their first dance atop the stars twisting around a wooden, centrally located dance floor. They were doll-eyed and completely entranced with one another.

Kylie knocked her knee against the hard wood of the underside of the table in her bored antics and winced in pain. The warm, spiced tea that she had been drinking was jostled, and the porcelain cup clinked as it did its own dance on the table. In the moment of distraction from her pain, it spilled all over the long, navy tablecloth and onto the lap of her emerald dress. The heat seared its way through the filmy outer layer of fabric and stung hotly on her thighs as it soaked through the darker, silky inner layer. Her eyes widened in shock, and she mashed her lips together to avoid squealing out in pain. She was sitting at a table with Mory and her parents, the king and queen of Arbore, near the front of the reception hall for the wedding of some local nobles, and the restrooms were not so conveniently located in the back. Her parents gave her slightly disapproving, although not surprised, looks while Mory stifled a laugh as surreptitiously as possible. It was a very rare occasion that Kylie could make it through an event such as this without causing some sort of ruckus. At least this time her knives were sheathed.

Mory had fallen into the swing of these parties naturally with his charming and witty attitude. He was able to create small talk and paint a smile on the lips of any noble who desired to chat with him. He was an outstanding people pleaser. Kylie, on the other hand, preferred to keep to herself and let Mory do the talking to outsiders. No matter how often she attended these large social gatherings, no matter the occasion, she never felt comfortable. Kylie despised these sorts of events and found herself to be incredibly shy and awkward. Keeping up a conversation about the weather only lasted so long before the talk turned to local gossip or herself which were two topics Kylie did not care for. She understood that the people needed to know her if she was going to be queen one day, but there had to be better ways to accomplish that than attending these abhorrent parties.

Kylie stood up, excused herself from the table as gracefully as possible, and weaved her way through the gossiping masses of people. It was impossible not to notice the large, brown, tea stain on the front of her dress. Kylie could at least admit that it had been a pretty dress prior to her accident. Its cut flattered her figure, and the coloring made her eyes gleam an even brighter green with Spirit. The royal seamstresses always did their best to make the dresses she wore comfortable and fluid enough to let her retain full motion. They even accommodated her hidden knives and provided her with pockets, but there was always this inkling in Kylie's mind that dresses were not for her. Maybe it wasn't so much the dress itself but the fact that if she was wearing a dress it meant that she was going to a social occasion.

The brown, liquid stain was spreading quickly, and it covered most of her belly by the time she reached the restroom. The shimmering emerald fabrics now looked matte and disgusting. Kylie shrugged, tied her long, golden hair back with an emerald ribbon that had been tied around her wrist, and began dousing the stain with water. What else could she do? She hadn't brought a change of clothes. Hopefully, she could convince the king and queen to let Mory and herself leave early. It would be dreadfully awful if she were to catch a cold on this cool, autumn evening in a wet dress. Kylie rolled her eyes in the mirror at her internal sarcasm.

As she was wringing out the excess water from the dress still on her body, she felt Regithal, the father that had raised her, calling across their mental connection that he had created when she was only a baby. She let him into her thoughts and replayed the evening quickly through her memories sent across the connection. She could feel Regithal's mirth and couldn't help but smile.

"I see you've maintained your reputation well, Ky," he said without a hint of reprisal. Regithal loved that she was better made for adventuring than party-going and was unashamed to let the world know it. It was a refreshing switch from the crowd that surrounded her at the castle. "How would you like to get out of that claustrophobic castle for a time? And let's say, go exploring another world?" he enticed her with his words.

Kylie exuberantly took the bait, "Oh, would I ever welcome a vacation from these boring burdens! What have you got in mind?" Over the next few minutes, Regithal filled her in on Scilla's plans to track down Kaitzen, and Kylie could feel the stress and tedium of the evening melt away as her mind filled with images of new discoveries and the start of a new and exciting journey. She must have lost track of the time because there was a hesitant knock on the door of the restroom. "Thank you for contacting me. I'll fill Mory in on the details. He should be just as excited as I am! Someone's here now, I'll speak with you later." Kylie hastily ended the mental conversation with Regithal before cautiously cracking open the locked restroom door and peering outside.

A wary-looking pair of eyes with a purple glow met her own. "Mory!" she exclaimed and flung the door wide open. "Come on in," Kylie waved her arms in a welcoming gesture toward the sinks.

He gave her an appraising glance before responding, "Don't you think it would be a little awkward if we were both caught in the women's restroom together?" Kylie's excited smile turned into a more thoughtful one.

"I suppose you're right, but I would like to find a place to talk with only you for a few minutes at least," she begged of him.

Mory smiled endearingly, took her hand, and gently kissed her on the cheek. "Anything for you, my dear. I had just come by to check on you since I was becoming a bit worried about how long you were taking in the restroom. Also, the king and queen have given us permission to escape for the evening, as the queen was quite certain that no matter how thorough your efforts were to clean the tea out of your dress, it would still leave an 'unsightly' spot." Mory had changed his voice at the end to mimic that of the queen's concern and put on a silly-looking proper face and voice for Kylie's benefit. Kylie couldn't help but giggle at Mory's mocking. No one was safe from his jests. Royalty or beggar, all were equivalent in his mind.

They found their way to a more secluded section of the castle and her excitement bubbled up again as she began to pull on his sleeve until he brought his ear down close enough so she could share the exciting news conspiratorially with him, "Regithal contacted me! Scilla wants to go track down Kaitzen. She wants to go to Tendyis. She wants us to come along with her!"

Mory slowed his walk and sighed deeply. The levity and joy on his face fell away, and he somberly ambled to an open window. That was not the reaction that Kylie had expected. She followed him over and stood beside him quietly and patiently to give him time to gather his thoughts.

As she waited, she stared out into the pristine night sky. It made the sparkling decorations of the party seem paltry. The deep blue of the sky was unobtainable by any human means, no matter how fine the fabric, and the twinkle of the stars glowing in soft shades of yellow and white was more gorgeous than any shining piece of garland. The cool breeze was more refreshing than any beverage served, and the flavor of fall in the air was more scrumptious than any dish she had tasted. The night sky was truly beautiful to her. Beauty was more than just a pretty shell; it went deeper. It invoked a warm, pleasant feeling of love and adoration in the beholder because of what something was within or what it stood for, going far beyond the superficial reach of the human eye.

Outside the castle walls, beneath the glow of the stars, was a freedom that Kylie had felt removed from for the past year. The outside world had moved forward while she had struggled and bumbled along inside. This was not where she was meant to be. At least not right now. She yearned for something more. The stars were calling her name.

Chapter 2

Thwack. Thwack. Thwack. Clunk. The sparring session continued. Although Dainn's usual fighting style utilized his own body strength with metal knuckles and wrestling, he had picked up a staff to participate in Elasche's training. The hot sun of the Diadust Desert beat down on his caramel skin, and his entire body was shining with a thin layer of sweat as he tightly grasped the wooden staff with both his hands, refusing to let it slide. The awning in the sparring grounds only covered the raised bench seating around its perimeter, leaving the central, sandy oval open to the elements. Evening was coming on, and the temperatures would soon drop to uncomfortably cool levels for those accustomed to the Mahashta heat.

Elasche was quick to learn the ways of the staff and even quicker in the wielding of it. She was attacking him with Sunlight on Water which he knew would be followed by Light-hearted Breeze. All the moves of the Ignet were named as such and transferred across the various weapon types with slight variations made to accommodate the weapon of choice. He defended against her assault, but it was not with the ease that he once could have. She was improving quickly. One day soon, she would need another more experienced staff wielder to train against, and then she could move onto spars with multiple opponents and multiple weapon types.

Her long, black braid was secured high on her head and flew around in a circle as she completed Whirling Water Wheel to dodge Dainn's Candle Douse. Her bare feet landed in the hot sand leaving small skid marks where they slid initially through the grains after completing a no-handed cartwheel.

"You should try to be less predictable," Dainn advised. "You tend to use a consistent pattern when you fight. Against new opponents, this shouldn't be an issue, but there will be times when you cannot vanquish your foe upon your first meeting, and they will learn from your tactics. Also, a craftier enemy may choose to scout you out and learn your fighting techniques and tendencies before engaging with you. Using the same moves against him as you did when he scouted you may lead to a quick demise."

Elasche nodded her thanks. He knew that she would take his words to heart and improve during their next spar. She was the most determined person he had met since…no he would not think of those days right now. It was incredible how often he was reminded recently of them though. Unknown to Elasche, she had opened a wound that long festered in Dainn's soul by joining the Ignet and selecting the staff as her primary weapon. Elasche knew all there was to know about Dainn, except one thing. It was a large thing. But the more Elasche trained, the more he wondered if she did know. There was only one person who could have told her, but would he break a vow to the elders over spite? Dainn did not think so. He was as devout of an Ignet as Dainn was.

"I see you've gone and trained yourself a little superstar Dainn," a haughty, condescending male voice boomed across the sparring grounds. "I'll be watching to make sure you don't let *her* down." He threw that last sentence as precisely at Dainn as if he had shot one of his arrows into his already wounded heart. Dainn's nose twitched slightly, but he forced his mouth to remain closed and his face expressionless. Lancet approached Dainn and Elasche with his bow slung lazily across his shoulder and a quiver full of arrows strapped to his back. He had a half ponytail tied high on his head leaving the remaining ends of his hair to freely sweep his shoulders. Lancet was taller and thinner than

Dainn but similarly toned and muscled. He looked them over appraisingly, waiting for a response that he never received, before nodding over toward a small section of the wooden, raised benches that formed a large oval around the sparring grounds. "You've got an audience this time, and they are growing by the day. Remember that, Dainn."

Lancet turned his attention to Elasche, and the tone of his voice acquired a hint of charm, "Elasche, I would be honored to teach you the skills of the arrow if you would allow me the privilege." He bowed his head slightly awaiting her response.

"Thank you, Lancet. Your offer does interest and flatters me greatly, as your archery skills are hailed throughout the Ignet, but for the time being, I will remain training with my most trusted, Dainn. I do hope you understand. I will remember your offer when I believe my skills could only be improved by none other than yourself," Elasche responded respectfully in the most politically correct fashion that only a princess could manage. Dainn was truly impressed with her. She had turned him down without having offended him or closing her door of opportunity at a later moment. He could learn a lot from her if he ever had it in his heart to speak frequently to people again.

"As you wish, Princess," Lancet straightened from his bow and excused himself, making his way out of the arena. Lancet was no dummy. He had understood completely what Elasche had done. That is why he had addressed her as 'Princess' before leaving.

"Lancet is a dangerous man to upset, Elasche," Dainn warned her when he was out of earshot. "His offer to teach you archery was most gracious."

"I know, but I did not like what I heard in his voice. His tone changed drastically when he was addressing the two of us, indicating there is more to the situation than I know. He had no real reason or gain to offer me his aid, and my instincts told me that… well… he may not be an altruistic person," Elasche leaned on her staff putting her finger to the corner of her lips as she often did while thinking. "When my instincts flag a person as a possible threat, and they offer me something too good to be true, I always need to take some time to consider the circumstances and consequences." Elasche concluded her reasoning and looked over toward the group watching them and sighed, "You'd think they'd get bored of watching me practice. If I were in the palace, I'd dismiss them out of irritation."

Dainn gave her a look that she knew well.

"Oh, hush now, you know I'd never actually do that. I know that it's not a normal circumstance for royalty to become one of the Ignet, and they are enjoying the show, seeing if I am truly worthy."

Dainn looked toward the group and nodded with a slight twitch on the side of his lips that Elasche had come to know as his smile, "I think they will be pleasantly surprised once you conquer your first trial tomorrow. Do you feel ready? Is there anything you'd like to go over?"

"No thank you, Dainn. I am as ready as I will ever be, although I will admit to being nervous. Do you think sensory extension is a good first choice?" Elasche inquired as they began walking toward the exit of the sparring grounds.

"I do. Especially with your Spirit talent in healing. It could give you further insight to help your patients. As you know, I can't give you any particularly helpful advice, per the rules of the elders on these low-level trials, but there is minimal combat in that one, and the danger level is low. I truly think you could accomplish it at the highest level." Dainn was twirling his staff absentmindedly like a long baton as they strolled. A part of him was excited by the thrill of the trial, but another part, he would never admit to Elasche, was worried about leaving her alone for its duration, no matter how benign it was.

"You'll have to teach me that sometime," Elasche said admirably as she watched him deftly twirl the staff. "Where did you learn that?"

"Hmmm… this? An old friend taught me," Dainn explained as he felt a rush of emptiness engulf him. He'd have to be careful not to let himself slip back too far into his past. "And yes, of course, whatever knowledge is mine, is yours as well. I will teach you whenever you please.

"After I complete the trial tomorrow then." A skip had made its way into her step as Elasche made her way toward the barracks they were housed in.

Dainn placed a weathered hand on her shoulder, "Hold up there, kid. If you plan on doing the trial first thing tomorrow morning, I'd suggest making your request to the elders tonight before turning in. Then you can go straight to trial grounds without any hold up."

"Yes, that would be a good plan. I am so glad to have you around to guide me through this, Dainn." Elasche turned her springy step in the direction of the Elder's Circle and began to hum a song from her childhood.

The Elder's Circle was not far from the sparring grounds in the most northern part of the North-Eastern quadrant of Mahashta. It was the piece of the quadrant immediately outside the walls of the palace which was devoted to properties controlled by the Ignet. The royal family thought it was best to keep them close and collected together. The Elder's Circle itself was segregated from the masses by a large open field of sparkling, white sand to give it a feeling of solitude. The sand field was dotted with yellow-green cacti with brilliant pink flowers. Small lizards could be seen scattering up the cacti when people walked by, and lazy snakes would sleep in their tall shadows. Once one had crossed the sand field, a wall of palms blocked the way, and a set of wooden swinging doors hung from two thin palm trunks above a white slab of stone engraved with a sleeping cobra. Once you had ascended the stone, you had to be careful not to step on the sleeping snake and speak softly by tradition. There was a brass hanging bell attached to the right door that had to be rung twice. Elasche rang the bell and awaited her call.

"The Elders acknowledge your call and open their ears. What do you desire?" came the shaking, yet strong voice of an elderly man.

"I seek your acceptance to attempt a trial," Elasche responded reverently. It was a tone that Dainn had rarely ever heard the princess use, but he was thankful that she had fallen into it quickly. Usually, people were speaking reverently toward her, not vice-versa.

"Enter then, young Ignet. We will hear your request." The wooden doors swung open with no aid in view. They looked frail and light enough to have been pushed open easily by a strong breeze, but if anyone had tried to open them without ringing the bell, not even Dainn's strength would have been able to coax them open a tiny crack.

Inside the Elder's Circle were eight plain, stucco houses with orange ceramic roof tiles immediately within the circular wall of palms. Dainn had never been inside one of those houses in all his years, nor did he know anyone who had. In the center of the grounds was a fire with a large, hanging pot being licked by the hungry, orange flames. Surrounding the fire pit, were eight white stones about the size of Dainn's head evenly spaced. On the side near the swinging gate, there was a large, rectangular straw mat that at least ten people could kneel on facing the fire. Beyond the fire, eight elders sat cross-legged, each on their own straw mat laid on top of the sand. Their ages could not be determined, other than they looked far older than anyone Dainn had ever met. The strangest part was that they never seemed to die or age beyond the stage they were at now. All of them looked very similar with their caramel skin and brilliant, white hair. They all wore white robes tied with red cord, similar to the required garb of the trial goers, and had various shapes and colors of clay-beaded jewelry draped over their necks and wrists.

This was only Elasche's second time in the Elder's Circle, and she seemed nervous. The first time was when she requested their permission to begin her Ignet training. They had thought for multiple hours about their decision that day. Dainn had even begun to doubt that they would allow her to train, but in the end, they had come to the decision that she could begin training. Elasche was not only a member of the royal family, but she was a Spirit wielder. Someone who could combine two magics, which she would become if she joined the Ignet, was a rare being and could be dangerous beyond the norm. Elasche no doubt remembered that day now as she knelt reverently next to Dainn on the straw mat before them, bowing to place her forehead on her folded hands in front of her.

When they spoke, the eight voices melded in a ghostly unison, "Speak your request, young Ignet."

Elasche recited the classic request format to the elders, "I desire to enter the trial for sensory expansion tomorrow. I have researched the books in the library to find the correct gate inscription, I have trained with others to fortify my strength for the trial, and my intentions are pure for the greater good of Mahashta. I will never use my knowledge against one that I was assigned to protect. I seek to conquer this trial to expand my utility as a member of the Ignet."

"We accept your request. Go with our blessing," came the usual response, but they continued on. "Dainn, you came to request something more," it was a statement, not a question.

"Yes, respected Elders, I would request that I accompany Elasche to the trial grounds even though I will not be entering a trial. It is my duty to protect her, and I wish to complete that task to the best of my ability. Beyond the gate of the trials, I will be powerless to protect her from the dangers of this world if I do not accompany her," Dainn requested determinedly.

The elders were silent for a while. Dainn assumed they must be able to talk over a mental connection and only responded when the decision was agreed to by all. He began to feel nervous beads of sweat coalesce on his brow fearing what decision the elders would reach. As the second sun began to fall beyond the horizon, they finally spoke, "Your request implies that you fear dangers beyond the well-secured portal gates but also speaks to your dedication as a protector. As we have never had an Ignet charged with protecting another one of our kind, this was a difficult decision with no precedent. However, we accept your proposal. Guard her well, Dainn." Their voices paused before continuing, "However, you may not follow her into any trial, unless you are attempting to pass the same trial as her."

"I swear on my role as an Ignet that I will protect her always, and I will uphold the boundaries you have specified." Dainn's forehead was still on his folded hands, which somewhat detracted from the vehemence of his statement, but it was there, nonetheless.

"Very well. Elasche, you may approach the pot. Your garb awaits you. Dainn, you are dismissed as well." With that, the elders disappeared one by one in swirls of smoke dissipating into the rosy-colored evening sky. Elasche stood up and stretched her legs from their crouched position before approaching the pot.

"Do not release the lid immediately when you open it," Dainn warned her suddenly remembering before she closed her distance to the pot. Elasche nodded in understanding.

She hesitantly reached out and grabbed the knob on the top of the lid and paused. She felt a tingling sensation on the back of her hand, but she heeded Dainn and did not release the lid. A rose tattoo formed in elegant calligraphy on the back of her hand before dissolving unseen into her skin.

"They have given you the key to the Rose Gates required to enter the trials," Dainn explained as she looked up at him. "You can release the lid whenever you wish now."

She returned to her original task of opening the heavy lid and pulled out a white pair of cotton pants, a white halter top, and red ropes. These were the traditional garb worn on the day of trial for the trial goers that was always given by the elders to an Ignet prior to their first trial. They would fit her perfectly. The garb gifted by the elders always did.

Elasche looked back to Dainn after inspecting the garments, "Thank you, for your request to join me. I will appreciate your company."

Dainn bowed, "You're welcome. I would worry far too much outside the trial gates. It was as much for me as it was for you. Come, let's go get some supper. You must be starved."

"Yes, I am." Elasche refolded the trial goers' garb and tucked it under her arm with a faraway look in her eyes. Dainn understood. The magic of the elders was mystifying, even to him who had seen it on countless occasions before entering trials. She would recover soon enough, and a little mystification was good for a person. He walked slightly behind her, as he always did, making their way back to their assigned barracks. There would be food saved for them from supper. The Ignet never had to worry about empty stomachs.

Chapter 3

That night, Dainn's worried mind refused to be captured by sleep. He stared up at the bottom boards of the bunk above his, the bunk that Elasche slept in, as the cool night breeze blew in from the ajar window, sending the curtains fluttering. Elasche had chosen to reside here as opposed to the palace a year before when they had returned from Arbore. She and her parents had gotten into a squabble where she had technically given up her position as princess of Mahashta and stormed out, although nothing was made official. Her parents secretly hoped that she would return after a while of living as an Ignet, but the lifestyle seemed to be growing on Elasche. After being held hostage in Arbore by Prince Sonu, her fascination with pretty trinkets and posh surroundings had dissipated, being overridden by an insatiable need for freedom. They had tried to convince Dainn to stay, but there was never a question in the matter. He would follow Elasche, whatever her decision was.

Usually, the Ignet separated the men's and women's bunk rooms, assigning two people per room, but an exception was made in their specific case. Along with the bunks, they were each provided with a desk, a chair, and a shared shower room. They could decorate as they pleased. All the Ignet housed in this barracks ate in a common mess hall during mealtimes, but there was always ample scrumptious food if people were to show up late. All in all, it was a comfortable lifestyle. Not palace living, but the Ignet were respected at nearly as high of a level and never forewent any necessities.

The bed and linens were usually quite comfortable as well, but Dainn tossed and turned for hours in his bunk before finally succumbing to a much-needed rest. His worry for Elasche in her first trial ran much deeper than his waking mind was willing to acknowledge, and as if to ensure he hadn't forgotten the consequences of failure, his dreams were plagued with nightmares from his past.

***

In Dainn's dream of the past...

A group of four Ignet, three men and one woman, sat at a table in a Mahashta inn before the rest of the masses awoke on their momentous day. On one side of the table, a man with a shaven head sat next to another whose naturally dark hair, a signature of the native Mahastians, was spiked down the center. Across from them sat a man with a thick, black ponytail next to a woman with her hair braided and rolled into two buns on top of her head, giving her the appearance of teddy bear ears. All of them wore the traditional white garments of the trial goers. For the men, this consisted of plain, white cotton pants with a red rope tied around the waist. For the women, this was the same, except they also wore a white cotton halter top with a matching red rope below their breasts. All were fit and muscular with an intrinsic beauty beyond the norm. Intricate tattoos decorated most of their exposed caramel skin, as these Ignet were the best of the best. Their skills were employed by none other than the Mahashta royal family during their residence in Arbore.

They had traveled in from Arbore the previous day through the traveling portals so they could get an early start, leaving behind other Ignet briefly to watch the royal family. An Ignet's training was never complete. No matter how aged one became, there were always new dangers in the world to counter and subdue. Today, they were going to take on one of the most difficult trials that an Ignet could attempt to master. It was known for its deadly perils, and they would be the first group to accept the trial at this difficulty level, but the reward upon completion was necessary for their deployment in Arbore. Strong Spirit users were abundant there.

The early morning desert light shone hotly in through the dusty window and glinted off the spoon Dainn was using to shovel his breakfast grits into his growling belly. A mischievous smile spread across his face as he angled the spoon slightly toward Lancet across the table, moving a circle of light playfully across his face before stopping it in one of his eyes. Lancet moved his head slightly out of the beam, so Dainn put it back. They continued this for a minute or so before Lancet finally caught onto what was happening.

"Mrryyyahhh!" Lancet howled as he banged one of his massive fists on the table. "Dainn, won't you ever grow up? I'm trying to get my strength for the trial today!"

Dainn laughed heartily as Lancet dug into his breakfast more furiously now, bringing it closer to his body as though that might shield him from Dainn's antics. Denna, Dainn's sister, sweetly leaned over and placed a kiss on Lancet's cheek which had the instant effect of calming the irritated man. "All will be well, my Lancet. You know Dainn, he just likes to lighten the mood of a situation."

Lancet's muscles untensed, and he grumbled something that might have been apologetic in Dainn's direction. Grymm, the man next to Dainn, rolled his eyes and continued to enjoy his morning meal. This all just made Dainn more excited. Before the trials, his blood always bubbled with anticipation and his emotions and perception were intensified to a significantly higher level. The thrill of the trial was intoxicating to him. Today, he and his party would conquer the mightiest of Spirit-wielders in the realm of trials and gain even more renown for their prowess as a team.

Lancet was their ranged attacker. Rumor had it that he could hit a mosquito mid-flight with an arrow from 100 yards. Dainn may have been the one to start this rumor, but Lancet didn't seem to mind so much. Plus, with his vision enhanced, precision sharpened, and mind stabilized with the help of his Koth –how the Ignet referred to the energy that was called upon by their tattoos– it was most likely possible, if he ever had the need to kill a mosquito in such a way.

Grymm was their tank. He bravely ran in and initiated all their encounters. He was nearly eight feet tall with broad shoulders and a barrel chest that invoked fear in the majority of creatures when he ran in bellowing his battle cry with his two-handed broad sword raised high and eyes ablaze with a battle fire. Usually, he was a calm, reserved man, but in the heat of battle, he would be difficult to distinguish from an enraged demon.

Denna was their healer, but she was so much more. Always the over-achiever, she was also a master of the staff and could hold her own in close combat with it. She was Dainn's sister, and between the two of them, they drove the morale of the party. Her with a gentle sweetness and happy giggles, and Dainn with his teasing and never-ending social energy.

Rosco, who wasn't at breakfast this morning, and Dainn were the primary attackers. Dainn with his physical strength, often wearing metal knuckles, and Rosco with his dual swords. Rosco was their unofficial leader. He was most likely up earlier than the rest of the group this morning, honing his skills before the trial or possibly meditating.

Dainn chattered incessantly throughout the rest of breakfast which did not surprise his friends. Dainn never lacked anything to say and could always fill the void of silence with teasing or unnecessary remarks to irk the others. Once the breakfast was cleaned from all their plates, the door to the inn opened and Rosco's serious face entered the facility.

"Are you ready?" he inquired with his voice that always held an air of authority, even though he wasn't that much older than the rest of them. The group nodded and walked out of the inn and into the sandy street. The sun beat down on them as a breeze blew by sending swirls of sand in mini tornados across their path. In order to get to the trial grounds, they would have to walk the tunnels. The streets were now lining with people eager to see the trial participants before they disappeared into their depths. There were faint excited whispers among the surrounding crowds, and Dainn would wink at some of them every so often to cause a bit of a stir. Never was their cheering though. That was a form of celebration saved for after they had completed their trial. Now there was only eager interest and curiosity as the group made their way to the tunnels near the castle grounds.

Two Ignet guarded the entranceway to the tunnels at the Rose Gates, and upon the white-clad supplicant's arrival, they bowed reverently. Among the Ignet, the trials were the most serious and important of ceremonies. One by one, the party members placed their palms on the rose symbol carved into the lock of the iron gate. Rose tattoos scripted themselves on the backs of their hands momentarily before the gate opened allowing entrance into the tunnels. After each person passed, the gates were closed so the next person could place their palm on the lock and gain their own entrance. Once they were all in, the gates creaked closed one final time. The sunlight cast the shadow of the gate's bars tall into the tunnels, surrounding the party, before dimming into near darkness.

The dim glow provided by the burning incense lining the walls was supposed to aid the trial goers in the light meditation that they performed before the trial. As required by tradition, the group walked in silence. This was when Dainn's nerves would start to eat at him. He was extremely confident in his abilities and those of his friends, but there was always that little voice of doubt that would plague his mind in the tunnels. He closed his eyes and deeply breathed in the incense. The sweet and spicy smell was calming, and he opened his mind to the inner peace that the Koth required. He felt a gentle touch on his hand after a few moments and opened his eyes to see Denna smiling up at him reassuringly. The look in her eyes told him that she would not only take care of him but the entire group. She was sweet like that.

Ahead, the tunnels opened into a cave filled with portals. Ancient Ignet symbols were carved into the stone arches surrounding the portals. Rosco, being the book fanatic of the group, began scrutinizing each of the symbols around the portals to find the one he was looking for. Dainn had many memories down here. He remembered clearly where each of the portals had taken him for his previous trials and what lay beyond their swirling vortices. Sometimes they went in groups, other times it was just him alone. Regardless of the situation, he recalled each moment of every trial. He had accepted years ago that he would never be able to attempt all the trials here, and for each arch that he had not visited, there was a blazing curiosity within his soul.

He neared one of those unknown arches and touched the cool stone reading the symbols around it to the best of his ability, "Fiery destruction." Dainn smirked a little. The trials were never very forgiving, or fair to be completely honest. An Ignet undertaking a trial could die in real life if they were not careful, and this unfortunate consequence had befallen others before him. The trial monsters never seemed to die completely. They could be vanquished by the trial goers, but when another Ignet came to undertake the trial, similar monsters and feats were required of them through the portal. Not even the elders fully understood the workings of the trials. All that was known was when an Ignet completed a trial successfully, a new tattoo drew itself on his body, and a path in the Koth within that person was unbarricaded allowing the Ignet to access his new abilities. This opening of a path was what every Ignet desired when they undertook a trial. The only way to know what path would be opened by a trial was to scour history books for reliable sources recording what was granted to them upon completion of the trial.

"Over here!" Rosco's voice echoed through the cave, disrupting Dainn's thoughts, and the party came to join him. The arch he stood near looked older than the others. The edges of the stone were smoothed over with age, but the symbols written on it were still clear, as the writers must have enhanced them with their Koth. The circles carved inside the arch at the precipice of the vortex indicated the number of Ignet required. This one had five, as the elders had told them.

"Are you ready?" Rosco addressed the group, turning to meet each one's eyes and accepting a nod as acknowledgment. "Very well. Ahead of us lies a group of Spirit wielders of an unknown number. They are battle-trained and have worked as a team for many years. Our goal is to subdue them. If all goes well, we should each earn the ability to restrict Spirit users from using their abilities to hurt us or those we are protecting. The better we do, the more Spirit users we should be able to subdue at a time."

Rosco finished his brief explanation and turned to face the swirling colors of the portal. He placed his palm on one of the circles, and a single, white, spherical light appeared in the vortex. Dainn followed his lead and another light appeared. The remaining members of the group placed their hands on a circle until five spheres of light danced in the vortex of color. They merged into one, floated toward Rosco's reach, and paused for a moment. Rosco raised his hand with five fingers outstretched indicating that he wished to complete the trial at the hardest level. He placed his hand in the sphere of light which then darted into the swirl of colors shrinking until it could no longer be seen. "We go, now." Rosco directed. As one, the group stepped forward into the trial.

Dainn's stomach lurched as it did every time he rode the vortex into the trials. This time, it spat him out into a large, grassy field that was filled with not only people but creatures he had never seen before as well. They came in all sorts of shapes and sizes. Furry, horned, small, large, hooved, clawed… any strange mingling of descriptions you could imagine, there were creatures of that type. His party had circled up to assess the situation, and Rosco determined that they were not supposed to be battling these creatures, they were supposed to protect them. The creatures were dressed for war and had weapons on their bodies, but they showed no ill will toward the group of Ignet.

In the distance, an unnatural storm brewed. "There," Rosco pointed. "We make our way there," Rosco decided as the party began its walk toward the sparks of lightning and crashing thunder amidst the dark, looming thunderhead. When they reached the edge of the rain, they knew the storm was fabricated. The storm front did not move but only circled around something. They could step into and out of the rain barrier at will, and it did not move with the winds.

Lancet's elbow glowed momentarily before speaking, "There are four Spirit wielders in there. Three are human. One is a creature that is thrice my height with the fangs of a wolf and the claws of a cat. Fur covers its entire body, but beneath it is a hard shell of protective skin that will be difficult to penetrate. My suggestion would be to take down the humans first, then all focus on the wolf-cat."

Rosco nodded while thinking, "That can be our going in plan. Be wary. We may outnumber them, but this is a level five trial. Do not let your guard down." With that, the group walked into the darkened rains and began to search with their senses for their enemies.

The attack came out of the darkness. A lightning bolt struck Lancet's bow and paralyzed him. Grymm jumped the attacker whose dark cloak blotted out the rain giving his position away. Denna buffed him with her Koth and unparalyzed Lancet. Dainn saw the tendrils of a plant with flaming tips and thorns begin to worm its way toward Lancet and called to Rosco who began to slice fervently through the vines while Dainn followed them back to their source and found their second Spirit wielder orchestrating the plant attack from behind a boulder. With a grunt, he began to pummel the wielder with his fists and bound him tight with his Koth. The resistance he felt from the man was incredible. It was beyond any power he had fought against before. He could not hold the bond for long and soon found himself in hand-to-hand combat with the man. It took much of his energy to dodge and repel both the man's physical and Spirit attacks. He quickly found himself overwhelmed.

The man jerked back in surprise as Dainn heard the thunk, thunk of two arrows sink themselves into his opponent's back. If that wasn't enough, one of Rosco's swords chose that moment to slice through the man's neck, splattering blood over Dainn's wet, white pants. Dainn always wondered why trial goers wore white for such messy business. The black-cloaked man fell to the floor as his head rolled in the opposite direction. Dainn dashed off toward where a lightning strike had shown him the shadows of the others. This man shouldn't be providing him any more trouble. He felt the soothing caress of Denna's Koth heal the worst of his wounds in an expedient matter so he could return to the battle. She was the best.

Dainn saw her twirling her staff parrying off the sword stabs of the same Spirit wielder Grymm had begun the fight with. Grymm was downed near her, and he knew she was attempting to heal him enough to recover while keeping the enemy at bay. Dainn rushed in quickly. When he was close enough, he saw the swords were dripping green. Poison. That's what had gotten Grymm. "I got this, Denna, heal Grymm." Dainn shouted as he dove into battle. The look she gave him was not a usual one, but she turned to Grymm anyway. Dainn carefully avoided the poisoned swings of the sword and quickly swiped the man off his feet. An exhausted Grymm stuck his sword into the man while kneeling partially on the ground. Denna had done her job well, again. Two down, one to go.

Dainn rushed off to find Lancet and Rosco with the rain pelting relentlessly across his back. He heard a scream and dodged a falling rock while managing to get stabbed by a handful of raindrops that had been turned into sharpened ice chunks. He saw Rosco parrying a slew of energy bolts being thrown from a Spirit wielder's hand. His sword movements were so incredibly graceful and swift that even the raw energy couldn't make it by him. Dainn reminded himself to praise Rosco's sword skills as "lightning fast" to the world once they were home. Returning the earlier favor Rosco had done him, Dainn ran in and pummeled the wielder's skull. The enemy fell to the ground, hood falling back to reveal the countenance of a blonde woman. A moment of guilt sped through Dainn's mind, but that woman had been trying to kill Rosco. He could not let any softness show now.

Rosco, panting heavily and limping slightly, trotted back to where Denna and Grymm had been before. Dainn followed. He didn't see anyone. He walked the paths of his Koth to attempt to locate them, only to find that walking through it was nearly impossible. He was met with a resistance beyond what he had ever encountered before. It was like moving through a sea of tar that was slowly suffocating him. His energy was nearly spent, and they still had the largest monster to slay. That sent a shrill of fear down his spine. He tried to call to Rosco. They could still forfeit the trial without death. The only penalty would be the embarrassment of failure. They just needed to make it back to the place where the portal had dropped them off. Those thoughts were fleeting, as Dainn had never forfeited a trial before, and the pride-driven force inside him laughed at the small, quivering form in his mind that wanted to go home. Dainn carried on.

A lightning strike illuminated the dark storm once more, and Dainn saw the hulking form of the wolf-cat through the rain. He ran over as quickly as he could on the muddied, rain-slickened grass and felt the sting of blood fall into his eyes from the ice rain he recently withstood. He tripped over a body in the grass. Lancet. His bow was strewn a few feet in front of him, but he was still breathing. Where was Denna? Was that her crying that he heard over the storm and howls of the wolf-cat? Denna never cried. As he neared the creature, he noticed that it would have even towered over Grymm. Where was Grymm? Rosco was valiantly slicing at the creature while pressing through high winds the Spirit-wielding creature had created for him to fight in. When Dainn looked closer, he saw that Rosco was defending something. A body…Grymm's body.

Dainn felt a slight surge of anger at Denna. Never before had she let one of their party fall, let alone two of them! Dainn pushed through the tar in his Koth to enhance his senses. Denna was on top of the grassy hill ahead, bloodied and in tears. He raced to her, grabbed her bloodied shoulders, and shook her slightly while yelling, "Heal them, Denna, NOW!" They need you. Stop this quivering. You've never been this way before!"

Her reddened face looked up into his, momentarily terrified before finding her strength to speak. "And you've never been like this before. You've never scared me or yelled at me so. Dainn… I can't heal them. My Koth is blocked. I have spent all my energy!" A new wave of tears flooded down her face masked slightly by the rain. "My leg, it's broken. I cannot move from here to even fight, and I haven't the strength to heal myself. I've spent it all on you guys. I've nothing left to give, Dainn. And Grymm…" she sniffled, "Grymm is dead. I tried to save him, but it's blocked. I've used too much. The paths are all blocked!"

Dainn stood up and roared his frustrations to the sky. This unwittingly turned the attention of the wolf-cat toward him. A tree branch was being hurtled at him in response, giving Rosco some time to get in a few good shots. The branch hit its mark, and Dainn's chest began to bleed profusely. "NOOO!" Denna screamed. Dainn slowly sank to the ground, and with his mind beginning to muddle, he yanked the branch out of his body. Denna reached out to him, her cool hands touching his warm, blood-stained skin. He felt something, a faint whisper of what used to be Denna's Koth healing the heart that was struck. He looked down at her once more into her dark eyes as she whimpered, "I'm counting on you. Protect her." Then she slouched backward in his arms, no more breaths to ever cross her red lips. Her once caramel face now seemed white and pale. Her eyes stared up, unfocused into the rain-filled sky.

Someone was pulling him away. He grasped at Denna. "Come back," Dainn whispered fruitlessly into the ears of the dead woman. "This can't be. We never fail," he whispered this time to himself.

He found himself thrown over someone's shoulder and unable to make his body do anything about it. It was Lancet. Rosco called back to them, "Go now! I'll distract him. You'll never make it back otherwise!"

Lancet groaned and limped forward carrying all Dainn's weight. "We can't leave them," Dainn's weakening voice protested.

"They are dead, Dainn," Lancet stated flatly. "We failed. We must go back and make sure no others are as foolish as us. None of us can access the paths of our Koth anymore, and you cannot walk on your own and won't be conscious for much longer. Rosco is only alive on sheer willpower. He has already taken a death blow to the stomach."

"But Denna!" Dainn protested once again.

"Is dead," Lancet cut Dainn off. "Because of you and your big mouth that never stays shut. I saw it. The girl I planned to marry is dead because of you, Dainn. She gave her last bit of strength so that you could live. Her will for that is the only thing that is keeping you alive on my shoulders right now. It was her last wish of me to save you, or her sacrifice would be for naught. I will honor that wish. You have no idea how much it pains me to rescue her killer and leave her body behind. Some brother you are," Lancet snarled through his uneven panting breaths.

Those were the last words that Dainn heard before succumbing to exhaustion and pain. He vowed to himself to never say another unnecessary word again. He also remembered Denna's last wish she had spoken to him… she was counting on him to take care of "her." She must have meant her most recent charge as an Ignet: Elasche, the royal princess. He would do so until his dying breath. Denna would not be disappointed in him.

***

Dainn awoke in a jolt from his troubled sleep. He hastily but silently got out of bed, covered in a cold sweat with his heart beating faster than the flutter of a dragonfly's wings. He stood up to gaze at Elasche in her upper bunk as she slumbered through the darkest hours of the night. She is so much like Denna…almost too much for his heart to handle. He will not let her down, not Elasche, nor Denna's last request that he protect her. Dainn clenched his fists and reached for his Koth to calm himself down before returning to his own bunk. He needed to be well rested to perform his duty well.

Chapter 4

Kylie kicked her legs back and forth on the wooden bench that was just barely too tall for her to sit on properly while she examined the relatively new lab. On the table in front of her, glass vials of various shapes and sizes lay scattered and tipped. Many of them had small amounts of strangely colored liquids present, and a few of those had dark particulates floating around in them. The shelves in the corner that housed a small library of books related to Mory and Anik's research had volumes slanted and horizontally shoved into nooks and crannies. Some were spread open to pages of significance with small dots of color speckling the paper and fire-singed page corners. Every so often, a strange chemical smell wafted in her direction making Kylie's nose curl in disgust, despite the window that Mory had opened immediately upon their arrival.

Mory had cringed upon entering the lab for the first time in weeks and had chastised Anik for his lack of cleanliness. Ever since they had created the lab in the Saliek camp about one year prior, Mory had ensured that it was tidy and methodically organized for the experiments that he and Anik had been conducting. They wanted to understand the genesis of Spirit and other magics to determine why they worked on some planets but not on others. This was the reason that Mory had fallen quiet when Kylie had told him that Scilla wanted to go to Tendyis soon. He was not ready. He had not found the answer to these questions yet and was hesitant to travel to such a faraway planet without the assurance that he would not be isolated from his Spirit. He desired a way to carry it with him if he could find one.

Mory's irritation with Anik had not lasted long as the red-haired man excitedly rushed out from behind a curtain separating the back portion of the lab. His slight curls spread out in an unruly mess about his head, falling in wisps in front of his goggles. As he turned his head from one side to another, peering at each of them, his eyes looked like they were changing sizes and bugging out of his head. His comical appearance, indicating serious hard work and a general lack of sleep, was impossible not to giggle at, but his pure excitement at his recent discovery was plain for all to see. There was a spring to his step and sparks dancing across his googly eyes.

"I have a theory…" Anik said as he was trying to contain his enthusiasm. "Lumirea! That's the key! The core of Krael has an extremely high concentration of that specific mineral. My powers seem to be augmented in its presence. I have a pile of it back here that I've collected from around the nearby mountain paths. Turns out, it is abundant on the surface too." Anik's usually black Saliek cloak secured around his shoulders was powdered with dust, and it sparkled as he swiftly moved toward them.

Kylie touched the rock on the necklace that Mory had made for her 19th birthday and let the warm memories flood her mind. That was lumirea too. She had learned that after Mory had found all Ghaleon's equipment last year and had been recognized as the Spirit Master. A rainbow of colors swirled across the mineral's surface in beautiful and intricate patterns. Kylie wanted to see this pile of lumirea that Anik had obtained, not only to see if she could sense its power, but simply to view such a large mass of something so beautiful. It must be absolutely stunning! She looked longingly toward the back curtain.

"I don't know whether to be jealous or excited," Mory replied. "I wanted to be a part of this discovery so badly, but

I seem to have stepped out at the wrong time. You'll have to fill me in on the details later."

"No worries, my friend. It's still only a theory. I've been itching to test it out more thoroughly. How would you two like to go planet hopping carrying a cache of this stuff and see what happens?" Anik tossed a chunk of lumeria up and down in his hand while issuing his proposition.

"Yes! Yes! I would!" Kylie jumped up from the bench and shouted. She was more than ready to go on any adventure that would get her out of the castle in Arbore.

Mory laughed heartily and added, "Of course! I'd love nothing more." He eyed Anik suspiciously, "How were you able to obtain core samples from Krael?"

A mischievous look developed in Anik's eyes, "Well let's just say there may have been a strange geyser of molten rock sighted in the Sentinels by a few fireling tribes. They seem to think they have angered a god of some sort and made it a sacred area that none of them dare traverse." He laughed heartily. "You'll see me in action soon enough. I intend to take core samples of the planets that we visit on our travels. I have a list that we can review before we begin."

"Can we see your lumirea collection before we go?" Kylie could barely contain herself anymore, and the request popped out of her. Anik seemed thrilled at her request, as it was an opportunity to show off his recent accomplishments.

"Of course, let's go!" Anik said with a swoop of his arm toward the black curtain separating out the back part of the lab. He disappeared behind it, and Kylie skipped merrily to the curtain with Mory following quickly behind her. The need for the curtain became apparent when she crossed its boundary. Dust that shimmered rainbow colors in the sunbeams that penetrated the windows hung in the air, refusing to settle. She coughed a little, waving her hand in front of her face to try and clear the dust from her stinging eyes and tickling nose. There was even a bit of crunch in her teeth! She understood the need for the goggles now. Anik quickly used his Spirit to quell the dust so that Kylie and Mory could admire his treasures while he found some goggles that they could use.

"Magnificent!" Kylie whispered as her breath was taken away by the sight before her. The lumirea around her neck was extremely pretty, but seeing the smooth rainbow rock in bulk before her was breathtaking. The colors would catch in the light, and sparkles of every color glittered across its surface. Anik had acquired enough of the rock that it piled to half of Kylie's height on the ground. Around the room, there were other piles of rock in smaller quantities that Anik must have been running tests on as well. There was a tiny pile of rare clarum that shimmered blacker than a lightless cave and broke into sheets when hammered. Hawthen was mostly dull grey and lifeless, but when it was wettened, it turned a bright blue. The lithia was a drab olive color and was known for being porous and light. Another interesting mineral Anik had acquired was flarium which was black and jagged until it was heated, usually by a fire, and then it turned a bright, crimson red. That had always been one that intrigued Kylie since her residence on Krael.

Kylie had always had a fascination with rocks and was easily able to identify everything in Anik's lab collection. In the past year that she had been on Krael, Kylie had taken up collecting rocks as a hobby. Krael seemed to have a much more diverse gathering of rocks than Thaer ever did, and their colors and properties were all far more extravagant and interesting.

"And I have to thank Kylie for my revelation," Anik began to explain. "For it was, as I was walking by the rock collection that she had gathered outside of her tent that I realized that all planets that we could survive on were made of rock… but not always the same rock! I followed that thread until I narrowed it down to a few minerals that seemed to have particularly special properties, and the rest fell from there."

Kylie smiled and shook her head, "You are way smarter than I am Anik. I never would have put that together from my pile of rocks, but if they helped you figure this out then I am more than happy."

Mory had gathered a handful of lumeria and was standing near that rock pile. He was looking toward another messy bookshelf in the back room, and it started to organize itself. "Hmmm. Not big enough. I think I feel it, but I need more." He spoke thoughtfully to himself. He wandered out the back of the lab into the edges of the Saliek camp where it began to mix into the wilderness of the Sentinels.

Kylie looked to Anik and motioned her head to indicate that they should follow Mory. They saw him stop when he looked up and saw a boulder high up on the mountain ledge before them. The boulder shook a little, began to levitate, and then slowly made its way down the mountainside.

"Remarkable!" Mory whispered in awe, then turned to Kylie and Anik, "Just this handful of lumeria, and I was able to lift that boulder with more ease than I would have without it! I wonder if it strengthens my Spirit or merely makes my use of it more efficient? Either way, I can definitely tell a difference."

Anik nodded, "It seems to be proximity and quantity based. If you are touching it or if there is a large quantity of it nearby, the assistance feels stronger."

"This is amazing!" Mory exclaimed. "I can't wait to try this out where there is no lumeria present." He paused for a moment to think before continuing, "This sounds like an adventure that Vi would love to come along with us on. Plus, her mirage magic could come in handy on strange planets."

"Good point," Anik agreed. "We should also let Scilla and Regithal know since we will be delaying their planned expedition to Tendyis. I think that if we explain what we hope to test, they will go along with our plan. Being able to access our Spirit anywhere will increase our chances of success overall."

“Makes sense to me,” Kylie said. “Have you told anyone else about your theory?”

“Nope,” Anik shook his head vigorously. “You two are the first.”

“Perfect! I’ll go gather the group and get our travel plans firmed up,” Kylie announced. She wanted to get this adventure started before anyone made her go back to the castle. Her life there really hadn’t been so bad. It just wasn’t for her. Her parents had turned out to be genuinely good people and were trying extra hard to help her transition into her responsibilities as a princess. She just didn’t want those responsibilities right now. She wanted to settle this score with Kaitzen that had been left unfinished and to be outside in the fresh sunshine with her knives and friends by her side.

The rest of the day flew by as Scilla, Regithal, and Zhannah were informed of Anik’s discoveries. Scilla had been particularly intrigued, but not with the lumeria. She took one glance at that pile, dismissed it, and gravitated toward the clarum. It was a small pile in comparison to the others, as it was much harder to come by. She had placed her hand on the pile, gasped nearly inaudibly, and Kylie almost thought she saw a tear glisten in Scilla’s eye. Kylie wondered what significance that mineral must have in Scilla’s life to invoke that reaction. Scilla had agreed to let the small group wander around a few planets as long as she was allowed to use the lab while there were gone, and they told no one else about their plans. Those were easy conditions for all of them to agree upon, although Mory did hint that he wouldn’t mind if she would keep the place tidy in their absence.

***

The moment Scilla walked into the dusty room, she felt it. There was a familiarity that vibrated through her soul, though it seemed oddly strange in many ways. It was as though the vibrations were at the same frequency as she recalled, except shifted. Anik had been explaining to them his revelation about lumeria enhancing Spirit, but upon her recognition of this feeling, Scilla made a beeline for the source. Clarum, Anik had called it. She knelt next to the small pile, and once her pale skin made contact with the pitch-black rock, a glimmer of an image entered her mind. It was fuzzy. She couldn't quite understand what she was seeing, but it was there. The familiar feeling with a foreign taint. She got the sick feeling in her stomach that had sometimes accompanied her visions and nearly retched over the preciously small pile of treasure in front of her.

Her visions… could they really come back? She had spent this last year hoping and praying, but this was the first real evidence that she had seen that she may be able to walk the paths of the future once more. She would study this clarum specimen. She would analyze it until she knew the answers that it hinted at. Her delicate, pale hand contrasted against the clarum's formidable, dark shell as she clutched it close to her heart. As she reluctantly placed the specimen she was holding back onto the pile, she noticed something odd. The previously black mineral had visibly lightened where she had touched it, leaving a gray shadow of her hand on its surface. Another interaction to study. She had to begin as soon as possible. So many secrets of clarum to learn and understand and not a clue how long she had to unravel them. She only knew that the longer she took, the longer Kaitzen had to wreak his destructive havoc… somewhere.

Chapter 5

The morning dew wet the boots of the small crew as they met next to a circle of boulders near the pegasus field. The suns had just risen, and the blue sky was dissipating the pinks and oranges of the morning into the whites of the clouds. The pegasi were munching on the sweet grass, barely noticing their presence, while Kylie stealthily rolled a few blapples into the tall sections of vegetation to pleasantly surprise them later that day.

Anik had given each of the travelers a bag full of lumeria. He had used his Spirit to condense the rock into much smaller pieces while still keeping the same magical strength. This made the bags only about the size of a small satchel that could fit in a single hand. Anik had seemed pretty sure that the amounts stashed in the bags would give them a significant amount of their powers on Blaet. Anik's "pretty sure" was as good as most people's "know for sure" in Kylie's mind, so she told herself that she trusted him.

Blaet was their chosen destination for the day. It was known that Spirit magic did not work there, and it was a neighboring planet to Krael so the Saliek cloaks would be able to teleport each of them there individually. They should be able to be back before dinner time. Kylie was a bit nervous as well as excited to start their adventure. Blaet was where her trial with Ghaleon had been. She had saved Mory's life when a group called the 'Syn' in her dream captured Mory.

The Syn had been against all magic users, and Mory, being the epitome of a magic user as the Spirit Master, had been a prime target on his visit to Blaet. He had been crippled from his loss of Spirit magic and was unable to free himself. Kylie's non-magical skills had been what saved them both in the end. She couldn't help but wonder if Ghaleon's trial had given her a glimpse into the future, or if it had just been an induced dream to test her character. Just in case, she had sharpened her favorite knife that was always hidden up her sleeve and placed an extra couple in her boots. It couldn't hurt to be a little extra prepared. She did trust Anik about the lumeria, but a backup plan was never a bad thing.

Kylie and Anik followed Mory as he pushed aside a boulder -with the help of his Spirit- and revealed the portal to Blaet within the circle of stones. All three cloaked travelers stood inside the circle, looked at each other, and then with a synchronized head nod they swirled their capes around their entire bodies, entered the portal, and disappeared from Krael.

In the darkness of traveling, Kylie thought she could hear soft and soothing whispers in her ears encouraging her to open herself to the stars and let in their light. "Open your heart to us, Kylie. The light will give you strength enough to share." She felt a strange strength blossom within her, almost overwhelming, before the travel darkness ended, and it dissipated to normality once more. Moments later, there was a burst of light, and Kylie felt a cool, refreshing spray of water on her face and looked out onto the backside of a roaring waterfall. There were trails leading to either side of the flowing water. She could see the sunbeams piercing through the water creating playful rainbows of light in the spray all around them and couldn't help but feel a joyful burst of energy. She started skipping along the left trail of water-splattered rock and clumsily lost her footing as her boot slid out from underneath her. Mory caught her before she hit the ground.

"Be careful, my love!" he exclaimed. "I don't want any of us to get hurt and force an early return. Kylie nodded and spent an extra moment laying in his warm embrace before he nuzzled her nose with his own and bounced her back onto her feet.

Vi gleefully popped out of Mory's travel bag and chimed in, "I absolutely do not want to cut this trip short. I've never been to Blaet before." Then her purple fairy shine flitted in and out of the smooth flow of the falls as she giggled in glee. After admiring the falls for a short while, the group finished walking up the trail to see the entirety of the Blue Lagoon where the Blaet portal was located. The waterfall poured over red rocks into waters of the brightest blue that twinkled in the morning sunshine.

"This looks like a good spot," Anik announced as he halted the group randomly. He placed his hands on his hips and surveyed the area around him before his eyes stopped on the waterfall. Suddenly, the waterfall split into two flows part way down. Anik nodded and pulled out a notebook where he started taking notes as he attempted different feats with the water and land around him. He had spent most of his time studying elemental properties, so manipulation of water, earth, fire, and air came naturally to him. Anik waved his hand around his head and told them all to start experimenting as well. Each of them knew their own individual strengths and limitations with Spirit. They could assess the effect of their stashes of lumeria by comparing what they knew of their powers on Krael to what they were now capable of doing on Blaet.

Vi found out with enthusiasm that she had retained her mirage magic which led Anik to believe that some of the core rocks on Blaet must be the same as on Krael. He began to fervently collect rock samples at varying depths from the ground beneath them causing large dust devils to swirl where he pulled his samples from.

With all their concentration on experimenting, the group hadn't noticed that they had attracted an audience at the shore of the lagoon. Sleek, green tails flipped periodically on the rocks while lithe, pale-skinned torsos curved up into lush heads of various colored hair.

"Mermaids!" Kylie exclaimed to the group while pointing toward the shore. She had never seen the creatures before, but she knew they existed on Blaet. She could not take her eyes off of the mermaids, just as they seemed unable to take their eyes off her group. Mory, Anik, and Vi all looked over at her exclamation. Kylie took a few slow steps toward the girls, and all but one of them splashed back into the lagoon. Her long, dark brown hair was matted with water plants, and her breasts were covered with a bandeau of large leaves woven together. Anik waved Kylie back, and she watched him turn on his "charming" look that he liked to use with girls. She had to admit, it was pretty good, even though a little dopey now that she knew he was doing it on purpose.

The mermaid watched his approach with wide, cautious eyes. When Anik got to within a couple of yards of her, he slowed. Kylie, Mory, and Vi were all as still as possible, unwilling to spook the mermaid and interested to see whatever it was Anik had in mind for the encounter. Anik started speaking in a soft, soothing voice to the mermaid, as one might to a scared animal. He reached out to touch the porcelain skin of her arm causing the mermaid to let out a piercing shriek, grab Anik's hand, and dive with him into the lagoon. Kylie gasped -letting out a breath she didn't know that she was holding- and ran over to the lagoon's beach with Mory and Vi close behind. There was nothing left of Anik except a swirl of water and bubbles leading into the lagoon. Kylie thought she saw a glimpse of the mermaid's tail flick as it plunged deep enough into the water that the sight of her was obscured.

"We have to do something!" she exclaimed.

Mory nodded resolutely, "We go after him. Do you know enough about water to make it breathable?"

"Yes, indefinitely," Kylie responded.

"Vi, you stay here, and if we are not back within the hour, use this to go back through the portal to Krael and bring help," Mory handed a tiny black cloak to Vi. She took it with a solemn face and did a tiny salute to show that she understood her duty. While this exchange happened, Kylie was sending status back to Regithal as quickly as possible using their mental connection so he could be prepared if needed.

"Good, now let's go!" Mory dove into the water first, followed by Kylie who checked to make sure her knives were securely in place before plunging in. The initial splash of the water was cold, but Kylie got used to it quickly. She had not known before now, but Mory was a fantastic swimmer. It took all of her strength to keep up with him as he swam deeper and deeper into the lagoon. He was like a fish, completely at home in the water. When her muscles began to burn, she saw what could only be a city in the depths of the lagoon. Bright corals grew in groups along the sides of rocky walls that formed buildings beneath the water. Anemones retracted and coiled their tendrils as schools of fish wound their way through the water-filled alleyways. The rooftops were shaped like large conch shell spires with green and yellow seaweeds clinging to the edges while flowing in the gentle currents of the lagoon.

There was a gathering of mermaids near one of the buildings. Kylie pulled on one of Mory's feet and pointed to it. He nodded, and they made their way over to the congregation using the buildings for cover as best as they could. Luckily, the mermaids were all very interested in their handsome catch and did not notice as Kylie and Mory approached. They were running their hands through his hair, poking his sides, pulling at his clothing, and investigating him with increasing curiosity. Anik did not look as frightened as Kylie had imagined he would be. Instead, the silly boy seemed to be amused and enjoying the attention he was getting from these mermaids instead of trying to escape them!

Kylie and Mory exchanged exasperated looks before trying to get Anik's attention and not the mermaids. Kylie sent a bubble over with a short phrase of sound waves inside, "Behind the crab leg stand," which was where she and Mory were hidden. With the way she had manipulated the water to be breathable, she could smell whiffs of the cooking crab legs which actually smelled rather appetizing. She and Mory used their powers to help guide the bubble carefully over to one of Anik's ears so he would be the only recipient of the message. When the bubble popped in his ear, he looked over toward the food stall and acknowledged their presence. Kylie waved at him to get over to them. Anik made a grumpy face back at her in response.

One of the mermaids seemed to identify this as Anik wanting food from the crab stand and swam her way over toward Kylie and Mory. They shrank back into the watery shadows, huddled together as best as they could behind the stand that looked like it was constructed of the wooden ruins of a shipwreck. The mermaid working at the stand placed her hands on some crab legs, and Kylie could hear a sizzle in the water near them. Without being able to see what was happening from behind the stand, this made Kylie wonder if the mermaids had their own special kind of magic. It wouldn't surprise her if they did.

Kylie heard a bubble-muddled shriek from the mermaid obtaining the food. She looked behind her to where Mory had been, and he wasn't there any longer. She looked to her left and saw his legs kicking from around the side of the shipwreck crab hut. She lunged over to grab him back to safety, but as she grabbed his legs, she looked around the corner of the hut to see that Mory had a hunk of crab leg in one hand and a mermaid grabbing him by the other. The mermaid won the tug-of-war contest without even knowing she was having one, flinging Kylie backward into her hiding spot once more. Kylie could not believe Mory had tried to nab a crab leg from the stand! She did not doubt that in his mind he figured he was 'borrowing' one. Now it was up to her to save both those boys from the curious mermaids. She didn't want to hurt the mermaids because they didn't seem intentionally malicious, but they also didn't seem like they wanted to let their new toys go any time soon. Kylie knew they needed to get back to the surface. Anything could go wrong and turn this into a worse situation.

Kylie frantically wracked her brain for a solution while remaining hidden. She saw a bed of tall, colorful seaweed on the sandy bottom and began to swim toward the school of mermaids through it. The slightly slimy tentacles tickled her body as she slid through what she supposed was considered a garden to these mermaids. When she neared the school, a merman with an air of importance swam into the waterway that the mermaids were gathered in and said something in an authoritative voice that Kylie did not understand. Mory took this opportunity to grab Anik and start kicking away from the mermaids. One of the girls near the back made a grab for them and unfortunately succeeded in snatching away the bags of lumeria that were tied to their belts. The mermaid had no way of knowing that in doing so, she had likely doomed her captors.

Kylie revectored her swim out of the seaweed garden toward the two boys, unseen by the preoccupied merfolk. By the time she got to their sides, both had been away from their lumeria long enough to lose their breath. She tried to grab each of them, one per arm, and kick furiously to swim upward, but they were too heavy with their weights combined. Her heart pounded knowing that she could probably save one of them if she let the other go, but she didn't think she could live with herself for making that decision. She tugged and kicked and gasped with the air that she had but made extremely slow progress. She pointed frantically to her bag of lumeria hoping that they could share the Spirit it provided, but both boys had already passed into a state of delirium. Before she had to make an awful decision, the weight off of one of her arms lifted, and Anik started moving toward the surface with the help of another human.

Kylie didn't stop to think or thank. She swam her hardest and brought Mory back up to the surface. She dragged him onto the beach, clear of the lagoon's water, covering him in a smattering of sand. She saw that her unknown friend was slapping the back of Anik who was having success in heaving out spouts of water and returning real air into his lungs. Kylie followed suit praying and hoping that Mory would recover as easily. After a few tense moments of unsuccessful back slapping, Kylie walloped Mory on the back with a sense of purpose, shouting "You're not dying on me now!" and water finally began to clear his airways. She could hear his breaths coming back in labored gasps and relief flooded over her. After she was sure he was alive and well, she hugged him tightly.

"Thank the Spirits you're okay!" she fawned over him. Mory was still in obvious pain from his chest and unable to respond with more than a grateful nod, so she backed away to give him space to recover for a few moments. She turned instead to their unknown savior and was taken aback by what she saw.

***

In another plane of existence, so close, yet so far away...

"Ah...young man, your time is soon." Ghaleon sat at a table balancing a teacup on his sword tossing it slightly up and down so it tinked as the clock on the wall ticked. During his lifetime, he had been very fond of tea, but in his existence now, it was a pleasure past him. His gaze moved from one of the many mirrors on the wall that showed images of the waking world and let it fall upon the boy that he had simultaneously saved and cursed sitting across the table from him. Ghaleon had taken to sharing Sonu's company since his transcendence. Sonu hid his eternal pain well. The pain that constantly burned his back from Ghaleon's sword strike was hidden beneath a stoic face. He was cursed with a half-death where he could flicker in and out of corporeal existence based on how long his life spark had charged. His life spark only charged while existing fully in the realm of ghosts.

"Where to?" Sonu asked, ever the compliant servant to Ghaleon's wishes, even though Ghaleon had made it clear that Sonu was a free spirit to do his own will. Sonu's own will was always aligned with whatever Ghaleon had in mind to purge evil from the worlds. For some time now, Sonu had been practicing his ability to balance existence in the real world versus the ghostly one. He had successfully accomplished many errands for Ghaleon while awaiting his time to help his sister and her companions once more.

"Kylie needs you on Blaet, in the city of mermaids, beneath the Blue Lagoon. Be ready to be submerged and grab ahold of a human." And with that short warning, Ghaleon snapped his transparent fingers and Sonu was away.

***

"Sonu!?" Kylie stood aghast before the semi-transparent being that looked remarkably like her deceased brother. He looked up at her and smiled with a kindness that he had never shown in the small part of life that she had known him. She didn't know if she could trust this version of him and was terrified that this was a trap of some sort. Her hand went to her sleeve, and she drew her knife while backing away to be safe. She needed to protect her friends while they were vulnerable.

"You're welcome, Sister. I aspire to be useful to you and your companions." Sonu said while bowing slightly before her. "My abilities," Sonu picked up a handful of sand with a solid hand, and then let the sand fall through his hand's transparent form back to the beach, "may be useful to you?"

Kylie was still staring at the stream of sand falling through his ghostly hand with mistrust when a mostly recovered Anik spoke up in between water-logged coughs, "Well it might be…cough cough…useful if you could help us gather core rock samples from all around Blaet. I'd like to get them…cough cough…from all over the core, but I can't traverse this entire planet in any sort of timely manner. You wouldn't happen to be able to move quickly about…cough cough…in some way, would you? I mean, you did sort of just show up here out of nowhere." Anik was pounding his own chest periodically to encourage latent water out of his lungs,

"I have my ways of traveling. Is that all you would ask of me? I committed heinous acts against you all during my lifetime, and now, I am determined to recompense through helping you on your journeys. Surely there must be something more than collecting rocks that I can assist with."

"Are you…dead?" Kylie cocked her head and examined his transparent appearance more closely, derailing the conversation temporarily.

"In a way. I am not fully passed on into the afterlife, but I am most definitely not alive. I am in a middling state awaiting my final judgment." Sonu responded while remaining as disarming as possible.

Mory's slightly watery cough turned the attention toward him, and he spoke with a voice that was confident and decisive for the group, "Those heinous acts that you mention are why we would ask a task like this of you now. How do we know that we can trust you? How do we know that this isn't some trap? Yes, you helped save our lives, for which we are grateful, but I do not have my confidence in your character restored." Mory's tone softened as he continued, "I have heard tales of ghosts and have seen them on occasion, though I have not seen any with the ability to return to the flesh. How is that possible?"

"A…friend…gifted me with this unique ability. As I said, I am not completely dead. I am trapped between the worlds of the living and dead until I have proven my worth to rest peacefully for eternity. You not only benefit from my help but so does my own soul."

Mory considered Sonu's words before continuing, "Succeed in this task and there will likely be others. And I do want to sincerely thank you for your timely arrival. We have our lives to thank you for. That does not go unnoticed."

Kylie had shifted the point of her knife away from Sonu as the conversation had gone on. She realized that he knew they were in their weakest state here and now, with only Kylie's lumeria stash to split between the three of them. Sonu was strategic. If there was a time to strike, it would be now. She started to think that he was indeed telling the truth, or else they would be fighting against him instead of talking with him.

In the silence that ensued, Anik added to his initial request with significantly less coughing, "Actually, you wouldn't happen to be able to get core samples from any planets in this solar system, or maybe some beyond? Having core samples from all the places we may go would come in handy."

Sonu nodded, "Provide me a list; I'll see what I can do."

As Anik began scribbling in his notebook, they noticed that a group of black-cloaked humans was approaching them from the portal entrance led by a bright purple spark. Vi had followed her instructions.

Before they arrived, Kylie looked to Mory and asked, "What in the Spirit's heart did you think you were doing grabbing a crab leg?!" Mory's eyes got big for a moment with the hand stuck in the cookie jar face, or in this case, hand stuck in the crab shack face, before attempting to bumble out some nonsense answer about being hungry and paying the mermaids back later as Kylie rolled her eyes.

Chapter 6

Anik had his goggles on in his laboratory, carefully brushing and inspecting the rock specimens that Sonu had gotten for him for the hundredth time. Kylie figured that he was just doing it to give his hands something to do while he was putting his thoughts together. There could not have been anything more he could have hoped to glean from visually examining the samples. He was pacing in front of a poster that he had made with Sonu's help on the lab wall. It had planet and star names as bolded headers with the minerals present on each planet or star scrawled with their percentages of abundance beneath the headers. When reading through the names of the stars, Kylie would sometimes feel something resonate within her, fleetingly accompanied by what she could only describe as soft singing.

"Hmmm, yes, I have seen nothing that refutes our findings. I firmly believe that we each can maintain our powers so long as we keep lumeria close at hand." Anik tapped the rock in his hand on the table in front of him in a quiet rhythm pulling Kylie out of her thought bubble. "It seems as though the more lumeria present, the stronger our powers are, so we should carry it around in as dense of quantities as possible."

"All minerals don't give powers the same way though, Anik, we must remember that," Scilla replied sagely from her spot on the lab bench hidden in a well-shadowed part of the room. "Clarum seems to have a charging effect. I can soak in the essence of the mineral and even store it for later if I choose. That must have been why I maintained my power here for so long, and how Kaitzen and I lost our powers on the same day. We must have absorbed the same amount of power before leaving Tendyis, and then it expired simultaneously. Someone with different powers may be linked to different minerals and acquire their powers slightly differently. Maybe we can map Dainn and Elasche's powers to a rock type if they are willing to visit us for an experiment."

Vi chimed in while playfully splashing water on the pile of hawthen creating radiant blue spots on the usually dull gray surfaces when touched by the water, "I think my mirages can span further when the hawthen is wet. Look how pretty it can be!" She splashed water more vigorously with her exclamation and giggled.

Anik turned back to Scilla after watching Vi flit and float about the pile of hawthen with showers of water flying everywhere from his sink, "You're right, Scilla, we should get Dainn and Elasche back here and see if their magic is connected to any of these rocks. That would give us another data point."

"It's settled then," Mory declared while flicking water off of his hands and face from rogue droplets that Vi had been splashing around. "I'll go talk to Regithal and arrange for messages to be sent to them. The sooner we get all the information we need, the sooner we can jump to Tendyis. Who knows how much destruction and pain Kaitzen has caused on that planet by now?"

Kylie noticed Scilla close her eyes and sigh ever so slightly at Mory's words. It couldn't be easy having your own twin brother as an enemy. Scilla had told them of her connection with Kaitzen after she had felt him leave Krael through the portal. Sonu was Kylie's brother, but she had never really formed a bond with him since she had never truly interacted with him before she was swept off to Thaer. Kylie sensed that Scilla and Kaitzen had been close. They must have shared cherished and important childhood memories together. Maybe the change in heart of Sonu would give her hope for her lost brother. Kylie tried to send waves of comfort and compassion over to Scilla with her Spirit. She had never really thought of using her Spirit to touch something as complex and intangible as feelings, but she did it instinctively. Scilla's visage altered to be perplexed before looking over to Kylie and smiling ever so slightly. In that moment, Kylie was sure that she would never fully understand the feats she was capable of with her Spirit. It was bounded only by her imagination.

***

Later that night, Kylie awoke to the sound of chirping crickets and croaking bullfrogs. She thought she heard something calling her name again. Dying of curiosity, she left her cozy tent and went out into the chilly evening pulling her cloak close about her as the grass cooled the toes of her bare feet. The stars twinkled above her in the clear night sky, and they mesmerized her momentarily. Kylie was tempted to listen more, but she didn't want to fall into a trap alone. She shook herself out of it and made her way to the laboratory to take a closer look at the poster there. She wondered why she was distracted so much by it earlier. As she started listing the names off one by one of the stars, Sonu materialized by her side.

"Dear Sister, do you realize that the stars speak to you? He reached his hand out to stop her finger from moving along the chart of stars to call her attention to himself.

"I had my guesses," she replied. "I just didn't know they could speak with us. It feels so warm and comforting when they call. Are they dangerous?"

Sonu paused thoughtfully for a moment, then spoke again, "As with many things, most are good. With the stars, nearly all of them are good. It is difficult for evil to corrupt something so large and pure, so from consultations with…my advisor…I believe you are safe to heed their calling and open up and listen to them. They are speaking to you in concert, together as a single entity, not reaching out to you one star at a time. This means that all the stars contacting you would have had to have been corrupted if it were dangerous, which is highly unlikely." Sonu turned to look at Kylie head-on, "Not many are called on by the stars, Kylie. You are truly blessed."

Kylie pondered for a moment if she could trust Sonu on this. He had been true so far since his return to them. It couldn't hurt to at least ask him more questions. She noticed him fading fast.

"I can still speak to you, but I wish to save my power for later if possible."

Kylie nodded. He had explained earlier that he had to essentially charge his substantial being in the land of ghosts, and she didn't mind if people thought she was talking to herself. That would be viewed as normal behavior by her to many.

Kylie spoke again, "When I read their names from this chart, I feel closer to them. I can hear them call more clearly. Do you know why that is?"

Sonu's bodiless voice replied, "Names have power. I suspect that you hear the calls of those stars that you name more clearly than others. Try speaking their names with kindness and trust, and see if your connection grows. You may eventually be able to feel them on an empathetic level if you are open enough to them all."

Kylie whispered in overwhelmed awe, "How can I learn all their names though? There are so many!" She shook her head disbelieving that she could accomplish a task such as that.

"You may never reach that point, but as with every difficult task, just start with one step at a time, one name at a time. I must go, Kylie; I am tired. I will be back when you need me again. Never fear. You know what you need to for now. Let in their light, if you can. They have ancient powers beyond understanding that can help you greatly." And with those parting words, she knew he was gone. She could no longer feel his presence in the lab.

Out of a whim, Kylie carefully rolled the poster off the wall and walked outside with it. She found a comfortable log to sit on and began partially unrolling the long scroll she now had of star names and began to inch her way down the list, unrolling with her left hand and rolling back up with her right. She opened her mind, heart, and soul to the call of the stars and softly spoke each of the names on the scroll well into the night. The more she spoke, the stronger and more comfortable she felt with the light that was being shared with her.

Another realm away, Sonu watched his sister begin to glow softly as orbs of light orbited her body before being absorbed inside. He doubted any full mortal could see the magnificent sight, even in the darkness of the night, since their senses were not as acute as his own. A dance of golden firefly lights flitted amongst floating autumn leaves as they traversed a green field from the skies above before being drawn toward and into this young girl, dissolving into her very heart. If Sonu opened his own heart, he could almost feel the hum of the star song as they embraced Kylie as openly as she did them. Ghaleon stood next to Sonu with a smile on his face, watching the magnificent show as well.

***

Starshine whinnied in satisfaction as Kylie ran her fingers through her freshly combed golden mane. Kylie had just finished giving Starshine's coat a good brush and massage this chilly autumn morning, and Starshine was adoring each moment. Mory had come with her and was pampering Knight beside them as well.

Knight had arrived at the Saliek camp when Mory first visited after Kaitzen had fled Krael over a year ago. No one had ever seen the brilliant white pegasus with purple eyes before, but he showed up in the middle of the night in front of the tent that Mory was staying in. His presence was announced by lots of clanging, and Mory greeted him at the tent opening with his sword point. To Mory's chagrin, his sword was confronted with a pristine white pegasus with a silver metal bucket shining in the moonlight atop its proud head and another bucket on its hoof making all sorts of clatter. He must have tried to raid the grain buckets in the stable before finding Mory. Mory had fallen back in sudden fear and then laughter at the sight before rescuing the pegasus from its dilemma. Mory dubbed him Sir Knight with his own sword that had greeted the pegasus. He thought it seemed a fitting name because Knight came to him during the night in shining armor. Bucket armor, but armor nonetheless. Ever since then, Knight always had a way of getting into some sort of comical situation but was never found far from Mory's side on any adventure.

Kylie could hear Knight crunching a blapple, and she looked over to see Mory smiling at her while Knight daintily licked his fingers on one hand for any remaining blapple juices that weren't already dripping down Knight's white, furry face.

"You know, you and Starshine both have gorgeous manes that glitter and glow in the morning sunshine," he said while giving her one of his winning smiles that made her heart melt.

"You are too sweet. I can't help but smile when we get time together!" Kylie exclaimed while beaming from cheek to cheek. "My cheeks hurt; they truly do!" Kylie added as she started rubbing them to show him what she meant.

Mory turned away from Knight and grabbed both Kylie's hands while looking into her eyes with his dashing, yet mischievous, smile and pulled her close enough to be wrapped safely in his arms. Her heart began to race as she overflowed with happiness at his sudden romantic gesture. She looked up and locked eyes with him, and it was like she was enchanted from the beginning all over again.

Anik chose this moment to come bounding around the corner into the stable, almost slipping on some straw scattered on the floor while shouting their names. “Kylie! Mory! They are here! Dainn and Elasche are here! They are sifting through the rock collection now.”

Mory pulled Kylie’s head to his chest with his hand behind her head and whispered into her ear, “Later,” before gently releasing her and swiftly turning to catch Anik before he fell all the way down from his rushed entrance.

Kylie felt extremely disappointed, but also incredibly excited at their friends’ arrival. It had been a few days since her naming of the stars, and she was wondering when they would be able to come to the Saliek camp and experiment with their Koth on the rock specimens that had been collected.

When she had told Mory of her star naming night, he had been skeptical at first about her connection to the stars. He did finally come around to think it was a good connection, but he was still worried about her and didn’t fully trust Sonu, yet. For the time being, he had decided that any help to their cause, cosmic or otherwise, was appreciated.

They made their way back toward the lab, and Elasche and Dainn were sitting cross-legged on the floor next to the pile of flarium outside. As it had been with everyone else, it was not difficult to find the specimen that was attached to their magic. The connection always found a way to manifest. The Koth wielders looked to be in a quiet conversation as they neared, but Dainn glanced their way and quieted, as was his way, before they approached within earshot.

Elasche stood with her staff, brushed away stray dust, and greeted them with a small princess curtsy in a cropped pastel pink top and poofy pink pants that came together in elastic bands about her hips and heels. It seemed her courtly manners were too well-engrained to have been entirely dismissed when she joined the Ignet. Her light-colored clothes enhanced her caramel skin, and Kylie could see the beautiful tattoo art beginning to decorate her body. She had been busy with her Ignet training lately. Anik was examining her even more than Kylie.

Elasche's eyes held a gleam of excitement as they neared, and even Dainn seemed more upbeat than usual. She quickly, with some awkwardness, thanked Anik for fetching them before addressing the group.

"This pile of rocks was labeled flarium on the diagram you gave us." Elasche motioned to the flarium. "We feel strangely invigorated when near it. Not stronger, but our Koth paths seem more open to our inner consciousness. We feel more free and less restricted. It's hard to articulate, but this mineral seems to be connected to us. Moreover, Dainn pointed out that he thinks a place the Ignet deem sacred contains, or may even have been constructed out of, this rock. May we bring back some samples to make a comparison?"

"Of course!" Anik promptly responded. "We have so much here, and we would like to learn all we can."

"Hold on," Mory said putting his hand up in a stopping motion, "There are other matters we should attend to before they take their leave." He turned to their visitors and began, "We have been making preparations to take a trip to Tendyis and find Kaitzen," then he continued to relay the rest of the story of their quest and preparations to them.

Elasche and Dainn had been there when it all began and were victims of Kaitzen's manipulation of Sonu, so they understood the root of the issue. They required some enlightening on recent events though, since they had not been privy to the preparations that were ongoing and had not been with the group for some time.

Mory concluded with, "I hope I don't speak out of turn since this has been Scilla's quest from the start, but I'd like to enlist your help to find Kaitzen on Tendyis and neutralize him if needed."

Elasche and Dainn seemed to have a conversation with their eyes before Elasche turned back to them and stated with resolve, "If Scilla would have us along, we would be honored to find and destroy the core of the evil that previously enslaved us."

As if on cue, Scilla was making her way toward the group, striding purposely through the cropped grass of the camp, covered from head to toe with black swathes of fabric to protect her delicate skin from the sunlight. When she was close enough to not have to shout, she said, "Regithal told me you were here, so I made my way over as quickly as possible. I heard bits of your conversation on my approach. A part of me would like to minimize the danger to others, but I can't deny that your help would be useful. You have both proven yourselves in the past, and it is obvious that you have trained even more this past year." She sighed deeply. "Let us not go in crying for his blood and retribution to begin with though. Maybe he is not quite beyond our reach, yet. Let us begin with open-hearted mercy."

The group gave her a skeptical look, but they all had a deep respect for Scilla and understood her situation. They agreed, with reservations, to not pull the trigger on Kaitzen until absolutely necessary, or unless Scilla gave the go-ahead. After further discussion on the details of their trip and what needed to be readied beforehand, they planned to meet back in one week's time at the portal in the Sentinel mountains that Kaitzen escaped Krael through to begin their journey to Tendyis.

Chapter 7

Scilla's nerves held her more than she let on externally. She had arrived early at the portal to Tendyis in order to make sure she was mentally prepared. The mountain air was fresh and crisp this morning, and the secluded atmosphere was comforting. Only the hardiest vegetation grasped to the mountain crags at these elevations, competing for the thin layer of oxygen remaining in the atmosphere, and it was rare to see even a bird announce its presence. This made for a blessedly peaceful atmosphere to blanket her nerve-wracked emotions.

She clung to a small piece of clarum that she had tied to a cord from the rock collection at the laboratory. It no longer had any charge for her foresight, but its presence gave her hope, something that in her darkest hours she would find herself bereft. A plethora of questions plagued her mind, but she knew that she would know none of the answers until they left. If the worst had happened to Kaitzen already, then all they had to do was return. If he was alive, she was sure that the trail he would be leaving on Tendyis would be hot somewhere. His desire for vengeance and, from his perspective, justice would drive him to extreme measures like those he took on Krael. She knew her brother well enough from their last connection to guess at that.

After taking a deep breath of the thin, but sweet, mountain air, she tucked the clarum piece back into her shirt and tried to re-focus. Anik had created bags for each of them with his Spirit that could hold many more items than indicated by their compact sizes. The others would no doubt stash a hefty supply of condensed lumeria or flarium, even though their investigations of the planets showed that Tendyis had close to the same composition that Krael did, with the exception of an abundance of clarum. She knew they would want to be prepared just in case they had to take a side trip or in case their information was wrong. Her bag was not very full. She hoped she could bring some clarum back for whatever good that may do her here on Krael…if she decided to return. That was the other big question that weighed on her. Her own future. Getting used to not seeing it was not easy. She had been exiled from her own planet, but what if circumstances allowed her to return? To have her sight back, to have her childhood home back, those were non-trivial things in her mind. How could she choose?

The rest of the crew arrived together through the makeshift portal that they had created from the Saliek camp. This disturbed the peaceful mountain solitude and brought Scilla out of her reverie. Kylie, bright-eyed and bushy-tailed as always, took in the scenery of the morning and smiled before giving Scilla a friendly wave. Scilla appreciated the spot of light Kylie brought to the group. She was talented and smart but didn't let the knowledge that she had weigh on her as many others do. Usually, that brightness was only carried by those without pain, those without the intelligence to see and understand the world, or even those who had others to carry their burdens for them. It was rare to see that light in someone with a heavy past and present who took care of herself, but Kylie was still relatively young. Scilla hoped that her strength to endure the pains of life with optimism would continue with her for all her years. That levity Kylie had was something that Scilla yearned for, but with all her years of existence plus her knowledge of the many possible futures, would she ever be able to let it not constantly weigh her down? The rest of the crew looked more somber and serious about the expedition that they were about to undertake. No one tried to bring Kylie's spirits down though as she took the time to kneel down and examine a small, brilliant blue flower poking its brave little petals out of the cracks of the mountain.

They gathered themselves together and talked briefly about their already pre-determined plans. Scilla knew the layout of the area where they would be landing on Tendyis, and from there, they would make their way back to the town where she grew up with Kaitzen. That is where she figured Kaitzen would have either taken up his base or taken down the town, indicating if he had survived his trip through space. The time that they would be arriving at the Plain of Portals on Tendyis should be empty of people if all was as it were the many years ago that she was there. They discussed the immediate use of mind shields created from Spirit or Koth upon arrival to try and guard against the future sight of the residents of Tendyis. They did not know if this would work since they had no way to experiment before leaving, but it seemed like a good precaution to take. They would be partly preoccupied while maintaining the shield, but if it did what they hoped, it could hide them and their intentions from Kaitzen.

Mory expanded Ghaleon's cloak so they could all fit within its confines, and slowly stepping in sync, they stepped into the unprotected mountain portal. Scilla felt the cold that she had experienced so many years ago upon her exile, but it seemed less biting. It could have been that she had grown older and more accustomed to discomfort, or maybe it was Ghaleon's cloak providing the extra protection. Before she could spend too long pondering, they shot out of the companion portal into a world covered in blessed twilight darkness. She got a few seconds to enjoy the lack of sunlight before she was accosted by simultaneous visions and a twin connection. She screamed out in anguish grabbing both sides of her head before kneeling and retching on the ground. She used tremendous effort to get her mental shield up while in extreme discomfort. She felt healing vibes come from warm hands and knew Elasche must have come to her aid. She was grateful for bringing the girl talented in healing along with them.

After a few moments of agony, she composed herself and tried to process all the information that had inundated her brain. Kaitzen was alive. She had felt his presence. An ominous cloud fluttered over her heart at that first thought until she moved on to the next one. Her prescience had returned! A great spout of joyous laughter poured out of her, and she fell backward into the cool grass, away from her pile of throw-up, and let that hope and happiness take her for the first time in many years. She knew her travel companions would think her insane, but she had to enjoy this moment for all it was worth. What she had lost was now returned. Both her home and prescience. Now, if only she could get that brother of hers to straighten out.

The cool, dewy tentacles of grass brushed her cheek as she stared up into the twilight day sky, and her exposed skin felt…well normal for once. She ripped off the access clothing she had swathed over her arms and let her paper-thin pale skin absorb the proper levels of light for the first time in years. She was home. For the first time in a thousand years, she was finally home.

***

A dusty, broken man viewed himself in a dusty, broken mirror. Shades of sanity flew threw his eyes as he contemplated his situation once more. His eerie inner calm and lack of feeling had diminished upon his arrival to Tendyis and had been masked by a crushing frustration bordering on fear at his utter loss of control over everything. Zen did not like Tendyis. He'd gotten his revenge, but he hated that everyone here was on par with him in future sight. He had gotten too used to Krael and the overwhelming power he had there over those who lacked. He wanted that back.

He knew Scilla had returned. He had felt her momentarily and began prodding. She and her companions had done something akin to raising a dark curtain to their possible futures, but with focus, he could catch glimpses. Two pieces of the puzzle that he saw in the glimpses stood out to him: clarum and charging. Those were his answer to returning to Krael. He had charged for about 12 years previously and that lasted him one thousand years on Krael. He couldn't count on another charge like that to last forever, and he would have to spend much more time on Tendyis than he wanted if he charged the natural way. Unfortunately, he didn't have a reliable way to get to and from Krael while ensuring his life to keep his internal battery full, so he would need to bring a spare battery. He needed to find a large, concentrated piece of clarum or at least a stash of smaller pieces to use when his charging ran out. Then, hopefully, the next time he traveled back to Tendyis, he would have the cloak of Ghaleon making travel back and forth less risky.

He focused again on that path of futures, twisting and traveling down dark tendrils in his mind, and he saw the possibility that he could have the cloak to make his return to Krael in the first place. How convenient! The Spirit Master was on Tendyis too with just the thing he needed: Ghaleon's cloak. He would try to find his clarum stash to ensure less frequent travels, yes, but if he could risk his life one less time to travel to Krael, even better! His treasure was coming to him.

He was currently lying low in an abandoned caretaker's shack near the Plain of Portals. He had been spontaneously changing places in order to hide better from the authorities after he had enacted his revenge. He knew that Scilla was very close by and knew exactly which portal to find her at, but he wanted to plan. A sudden, reckless ambush wasn't his style, which was part of why he hated Tendyis. Thankfully, he now knew from his sister's attempts that mind cloaks could haze other's views of his future, so he went to rummaging in the bag of artifacts that he had brought with him from his horde on Krael to find something to suit his needs in the meantime.

***

When Scilla finally calmed down enough, she sat up and took in the surrounding scenery. The Plain of Portals at least seemed unchanged. The same thrum of energy vibrated through her at the golden base of the swirling, colored portal, just as it did so many years ago. Perfectly circular portals dotted the otherwise vacant field, with gleaming golden perimeters in the soft daylight, akin to moonlight on Krael. The group was watching her, and Elasche had helped her sit up when she tried. She apologized for the sudden outburst, and the group seemed to be hiding little smiles. She couldn't really blame them. She had never let emotion take her that way before in front of them, but she had also never felt so liberated before either. If only Andolin could see her now. Her deceased love had always been exulted to see her happy. Maybe he could see her, and that thought made her smile even more.

The group still watched her, and she realized that they were waiting for her to take the lead now that they had made it to Tendyis. It made sense. This was her home planet. She would know the terrain best, and she would know their possible adversaries best, as well. Regardless, the burden began to weigh on her. She was used to acting alone or orchestrating from the sidelines, not leading a group outright, but she would do it.

Scilla stood up on her own, even though Elasche was there to help, composed herself, and stuffed her extra clothing into her satchel. She waved her hand in a general direction and began striding, "This way to my old hometown. It shouldn't be far. We should be able to walk there before the day's end."

"Are you sure you don't need some time to refresh or relax before we go?" Elasche inquired with concern, jogging slightly to catch up.

Scilla paused and put her hand on Elasche's shoulder, favoring her with a smile, "It is sweet of you to ask, dear, but no, I do not require any more time. I feel better than I have in many years. Let us continue our journey for now, I will let you know if I don't feel well again. Thank you again for caring for me just now."

Elasche seemed appeased by her response and dropped back slightly to the rest who were following Scilla. They walked on for some time across the vast field of portals before Mory froze and motioned for them to stop. "I've been hearing the slight crunching of footsteps through grass, and I could have sworn I heard the grunt of a horse nearby. Does anyone else sense anything?"

Anik, using his prowess over the elements, swirled the winds in his direction and confirmed a horsey scent from the open field nearby which looked entirely empty. Scilla had a thought. "Vi, you can see the other creatures and items that are invisible when you use your mirage magic, correct?

Vi flew happily from Mory's shoulder to Scilla in her usually bouncy manner, throwing a loop-the-loop in for fun. "Absolutely, Scilla! Let me go ahead and take a looksee for you." And with that, Vi blinked out of existence while they all waited with bated breath.

After a few minutes, Vi reappeared a few inches from where she disappeared and started to relay her experience excitedly. "Black and grey horses! A small herd of them is grazing on the grass nearby. They are smaller than the pegasi on Krael, and they seem shy. I tried to say "hi" to one of the ones on the edge, but she eyed me in a distrustful way and turned her rump toward me. Can you believe the audacity!?"

Scilla smiled at the energetic little fairy emitting a shimmering purple essence in front of her, “Thank you, Vi.” Then she addressed the group, “These are what are known as the ‘night mares’ on this planet. They are harmless, shy creatures, but they are feared by some because of their ability to become invisible, which appears to be the same as, or at least related to, Vi’s mirage magic. Well, that, and they tend to congregate in places where terrible memories have been made, even though they can survive anywhere on the planet. It is theorized that they feed on those dreadful memories. Some say they cleanse the fear from them, others say they bask in it. No one has been able to tell for sure. I, for one, believe they cleanse the fear.”

“Do you think we could ride them if we befriended them?” Mory asked while squinting in the direction that Vi had indicated the night mares were residing, hoping to catch a glimpse of one of them by accident.

“You could,” Scilla responded while gaining a far-away look in her eyes. “I have when I was a child, but gaining their trust is not the easiest. For days, I sat food out behind my house when I saw a herd, and I would go outside and sit on my porch watching them, when they were visible, humming a soothing song my mother had taught me. One day, one of them approached me, and I was able to befriend her. We would escape together sometimes to be away from our worlds.” At the thought of her mother and the long-lost memory of her furry friend, Scilla felt her voice catch. She hadn’t thought she would recall those memories ever again. They had been lost to the flow of time until now, and she turned them over and cherished them in her mind like a subtly sweet treat slowly melting in her mouth. She began quietly humming the soothing song once more after all those years.

“Another day then,” Mory resigned as they continued their trek across the twilight planet.

Chapter 8

Battered and broken shells that once belonged to wooden buildings were strewn across the place that was once Scilla's hometown. Remnants of everyday life dotted the wooden ruins in a grotesquely eerie fashion: cloth clothing torn and charred, a tire swing twisted in its own rope, broken glass cutting into the dirt, and wilted people wandering around listlessly or tucked into crevices of the ruins that could still provide a semblance of shelter. The devastation of the scene was mirrored in Scilla's heart, but she refused to let it beat her down. Instead, she looked on with determination and instinctively started walking down what used to be a road toward her old house before something caught her ear.

A mellifluous melody distinctly out of place was coming from the wreckage of the old stable. There was something slightly off about the sound, but that oddness in the melody serenaded the scenery perfectly. As she listened, she walked closer and saw a boy in tattered clothes with an old, splintering lute playing in the rubble. One of the strings on his ragged instrument was broken, which was the cause of the oddness in the sound, but he continued playing regardless.

Scilla stopped her approach and began to truly listen to the music with closed eyes and an open heart. It was transformative in feeling. She could hear the sounds of a soothing rain cleansing the streets and a soft breeze blowing away the frothing dust looming in the sky. The rains churned for a while before the sun peeked out of the clouds, bringing bright butterflies and the beautiful light of hope to the little town with a forgotten name. She could almost hear the sounds of children playing and the hearty laugh of a couple having a peaceful stroll together while the ting of a blacksmith's hammer worked fruitfully in the background.

The song quieted, and Scilla opened her eyes once more. The town was the same pitiful pile of rubbish that they had entered. It was nothing like the boy's dream painted in the sound of his instrument. His talent was beyond anything she had heard before in her many years. It was a good omen for the town that dreams like that still existed in its people, even in its currently dreary state. When she looked closer, she could see that the wilted people maybe weren't as wilted as they had first seemed to her upon arrival. They were deliberately picking up the rubble. They were rebuilding, however agonizing slow, the town that was once theirs. They had chosen not to abandon it.

Mory had made his way over to the boy and was speaking quietly with him. He placed his hands on the broken lute, and the old instrument came back to its original glory. The lute's strings snapped back into place, and the painting on its wooden face came back to life as a herd of night mares with a swirl of pink blossoms flowing out behind them took shape from the dust. The boy looked on in awe at the transformation, and a tear escaped from one of his eyes before he hugged Mory in thanks. Mory waved to the boy before coming back toward Scilla. She heard the boy fervently start playing once more with even more beauty than before.

"His talent is without precedence," Scilla stated as Mory returned.

Mory turned to her with a faraway look in his eyes, "I know. I could see his dreams for this town in the music he was playing. I don't know if there was a magic to his music beyond its beauty to begin with, but now when he plays his songs will become reality, to a certain extent. I had read many books about music, and I know how to repair wooden structures and sweep away dust. Now, when he plays his instrument, the town will begin to rebuild itself, just like the music in his dream that he was playing."

Scilla had never thought to use her Spirit in that way before, but that was why Mory was the Spirit Master. "You are brilliant, Mory. He will cherish that gift you gave him forever." She watched as the boy's song swept away the dirt around him and stones that had once been foundation began straightening themselves. He played so seriously and fervently although the sound of his music was bright and happy. Hope was certainly not lost for this town.

Mory combed his fingers through his messy blonde hair as he replied, "I asked him how it was that his music was so happy and uplifting when his home had been demolished. He told me, 'You can't wait for life to be easy to be happy.' And just like that, I knew I had to help him."

Scilla nodded. She had never gotten to see this side of her town before. Maybe the people here had changed over the generations, or maybe it had taken utter devastation to bring the goodness out of them once more.

Inspired by the musician boy, the group spent the rest of the evening contributing to the rebuilding of the town while asking residents about the catastrophe that had happened. It sounded like Kaitzen had never even shown his face. He must have utilized one of his relics to create a tornado-like storm to rip through the town.

Scilla wondered if anyone knew it was him. Their names and images would have been recorded in the town's library as exiles to be eradicated if they ever returned, and there were not many people in the book. If they had been living normal lifespans, they would have been deceased by now, even on Tendyis which had slightly longer life expectancies than Krael. It didn't seem likely that Kaitzen would have been chased or caught, but if someone had been following the paths of the future at the time Kaitzen arrived on the planet, his presence could have made a large blip in their prophecies from his sudden existence and driving urge for vengeance. The list of suspects from that would be small if they consulted the exile listing from this town. No one from her town would have been trying to see the future though, if they believed in the same guiding principles as they had been when she resided here. The gathering of people here had been vehemently against viewing the future and did their best to live their lives spontaneously. But an outsider could have seen this possibility and investigated out of curiosity. So many possibilities.

Scilla decided to use her future sight intentionally for the first time since their arrival. Since she was not being overcome by a sudden prophecy, the vomiting sickness that usually plagued her shouldn't take effect, and the results shouldn't be as cryptic, but the experience could leave her woozy. Knowing this, she sought out a quiet place in the field that her house had once overlooked and asked Elasche to accompany her. Dainn came with them as well. Kylie, Mory, and Anik could continue to help and investigate the town on their own for a while.

When they were just far enough away from the village, Scilla sat down in the grass and put her cloth swathes back over her arms since the evening chill was starting to set in as the dim sun of their solar system, Larian, set. She closed her eyes and released her mind from her physical senses. She let it hang for a second, bobbing in indecision before giving herself a nudge down a tendril that she thought she felt Kaitzen's presence down. The little nudge sent her mind racing down tendrils faster than any form of transportation known, including teleportals. The speed alone could have made someone nauseous, and many were the first few times they traveled the paths of the future, but the bombardment of the brain with all the information was even more stomach-churning than the speed. She saw images of Kaitzen razing the entirety of Tendyis, though those paths were few and far between. She saw images of Kaitzen attempting to return to Krael in various fashions: with and without Ghaleon's cloak, with and without clarum, forced from a chase and on his own, and other variants. She saw his death. She saw his capture. She saw an endless number of possibilities, but the paths that repeated most frequently were those of him returning to Krael sooner than later, and in all instances, he knew of Scilla's presence. Meaning something they had done had already tipped him off. That was valuable information to have learned. He was planning something to encounter them. Beyond Tendyis she could see nothing, as was always true with her powers. She could not see anything beyond the planet on which she was currently located.

Scilla returned her mind to her physical senses and felt Elasche holding her hand. "How long have I been gone?"

Elasche responded, "A little less than an hour. Long enough for Dainn to have gone off exploring and come back with some questions on the area."

Scilla nodded. She had traveled down an incredible number of time trails in her mind in order to get good statistics on the possible futures. It seemed like the most likely one was Kaitzen's return to Krael. It was possible that they could defeat him here or even turn his allegiances over to their side, but the odds were against them in the current time stream. She wished she could see the time streams on Krael. Maybe there was more information to be had there. Maybe they would be more likely to defeat him or persuade him on that planet. She wouldn't know until she returned, and Kaitzen would have to be on that planet as well for her to get a reading on him. Maybe one of her more cryptic sudden visions would overtake her with a more concrete answer if she could solve the puzzle presented to her in time.

Scilla turned to Dainn who was sitting cross-legged in the grass staring at the terrain of the open field intently, as if examining and scrutinizing every hill, every tree, and possibly even every blade of grass. His solemnity perplexed her, and he rarely asked for favors. He always had a menacing air about him with his tattoo-covered body, bulging muscles, and expressionless face, even when sitting relatively relaxed in the company of friends. Scilla was very curious as to the inquiries of the usually silent man, "I will answer anything that I can, please ask away."

Dainn looked to her and asked, "Is there any significance to this place? You mentioned that the night mares would congregate here, implying that terrible memories were made on this terrain. This place reminds me of somewhere I've been before, and I must hear what you know of it."

Dainn's stare was so intense and intimidating as he spoke that Scilla fumbled a bit while searching her mind for the information he requested. "There was a battle here eons ago. During the reign of Ghaleon, evil monsters known as 'splicers' would attack the sentient planets of the universe. They would attack not only in the physical sense but also in far worse ways. Their appearance would warp the minds and hearts of good creatures with vile manipulation through whispers in dreams or visits in reality. Once kind and courteous creatures would turn selfish and vengeful. Good hearts would steal and lie when they used to give and honor. This harbored more distrust amongst the populace, and the evil in each being's heart would grow even if they were untouched by the splicer and only influenced by their family, friends, and acquaintances that were originally affected by its presence. Only those who could find the strength to love and show kindness and bring happiness despite being drowned in the darkness could thwart the contagious evil brought by the splicers."

"Splicers could alter their forms to any they desired and could spend untold amounts of time in the space between portals and planets, therefore avoiding the future sight of the beings on Tendyis. This was also how they gained their name 'splicers' since they could travel without consequence through the void, essentially connecting together separate planets with ease."

"At the insistence of Ghaleon, various factions of magic-wielding creatures banded together in order to defeat them. At this particular battlefield, the beings with future sight did their best to isolate the location of one such splicer known as Ramanatra. Spirit wielders were sent into the storm cloud being generated by Ramanatra in his rage to take him down. They did not return in a timely fashion, so they sent the Ignet in after them. The Ignet found the lost Spirit wielders, but their minds had been altered due to the enemy. The Ignet captured their allies and dispelled the spell cast over them. The Ignet and Spirit wielders combined their powers in order to take Ramanatra down. This was the first such battle in the known universe where magic beings from different planets combined their powers, and it was through that cooperation that the rest of the splicers were able to be defeated. Details of this battle and others can be found in the 'Legends, Myths, and Tales of the Universe' book that I gave to Kylie when this all began. My guess would be that she has it in her bag if you're interested in reading more of that encounter or other battles."

Dainn's usually stoic face seemed unable to cope with whatever emotions he was currently experiencing. Both Scilla and Elasche watched him cautiously waiting for a reaction. "Together was the answer," was all he managed to say while shaking his head slowly and letting the tension out of his balled fists.

***

The truth of the matter hit Dainn hard, and he couldn't understand how they had faltered so badly. His frustration battled ruthlessly with the peace and balance of his inner Koth until his Koth finally won out. He wondered now if all the portals beyond the Rose Gates were tied to historic events, or if this one was a singularity. Could it be possible that the portals were miniature time warps taking the participants back to re-enact historic events? The likeness of the battlefield before his eyes was too similar to be a coincidence, and it *felt* the same when he walked over it.

He knew what he had to do. He had to go back to the portal challenge that his team had failed and conquer it. Conquer it together with the Spirit wielders. He couldn't abandon his friends here on Tendyis now though. That would be making a similar mistake as he did before. He would wait for the opportune time to go back and hopefully right the wrongs of so many years ago. He knew he shouldn't hurry into this, even though something inside urged him forward. He needed to complete his task at the present and figure out a way to convince Lancet to come with him. He knew Lancet would be as invested in this endeavor as he was if Dainn could find the right words for him. Blessed Koth...he had hope for Denna and his lost friends again!

***

Sonu looked on as he always did, a partial realm away, and turned to Ghaleon's ethereal existence. "Do the splicers still exist? Will Kylie need to confront them before this all ends?"

Ghaleon held the mist of a cloud in the center of his hands cupped into a sphere while poking his ghostly fingertips into the mist one by one as he often did when he was idling or pondering. "The splicers no longer exist in a physical sense, young one. I made sure of that. Yet, the after-effects of their presence still remain." Ghaleon squished the cloud together in his hands, letting the mist squeeze through his fingers before moving them back and encircling the misty cloud sphere with his hands once more. "This was my mistake. The Greatest Spirit warned me that evil was not yet vanquished when I had quelled the splicer's physical forms, but I was selfish and wanted so badly to be reunited with my family instead of continuing on in a mortal sense. The seeds of mistrust, hatred, fear, pain, and more live on in the hearts of the creatures of the universe. As Scilla mentioned, the only way to combat this is with love and kindness. The tainted creatures need their hearts healed completely from the evil seeds of the splicers before anyone can say all evil has been removed from the worlds. Just as kindness begets kindness, evil begets evil. We all live in an interconnected circle, as such, we must help bring each other back from the edge of darkness within our own hearts when needed."

"You, yourself, Sonu, succumbed to the darkness. You know how heavy a burden it is. You know how difficult it is to lift. Your own partial death and seeing all the possibilities of good in your life had you taken other paths was required for you to see the light within yourself once more. Reaching the ears of the tainted ones is not easy. Bringing them back to the light is the most difficult problem I have encountered. Bringing everyone back is not something one person can do, but all of us need to work together every day to vanquish the evils around us with kindness."

"My hope is that the magic within the Spirit Master is always strong enough to keep the evil at bay so that they can be a good model. If there is always at least one good heart in the universe, others may come to emulate them. I do not know the answer to all the questions of evil, but through my years of pondering, kindness is my best answer. Even if it is the wrong answer, it isn't detrimental to try to always be kind."

Sonu nodded in understanding, feeling the pain of the thorn in his back that was plagued to throb endlessly until he earned a full death by helping his sister. He would not fall again to what he once was. He would do his best not to let others fall either. Ghaleon disappeared to likely be with his family. Sonu had nowhere to go or anything to do but watch the world of the living in his partial existence and think.

Chapter 9

Mory's conversation with the librarian had gone fairly well. He had gotten over to her as the white sun, Larian, began to rise, creating a layer of purple haze in the sky dotted with lavender clouds before fading away into the deep blue of space. This was when the other town folk had said the older lady was the most amicable. She had gotten grumpy and unpredictably rude with her words as she aged, but once Mory had sifted through the myriad of colorful insults, which were honestly rather creative, she had a wealth of knowledge for sharing. Mory was thankful that he had spent all those years under Scilla's tutelage because one of the languages which she had harped on him to learn was that of her hometown under the guise of a long-lost language from ages ago. Not only did he get to learn much information from the librarian here on Tendyis this morning from the fruit of his previous studies, but he could understand the insults well enough to find them amusing which left him with a satisfied feeling to start the day.

The town, known as Patten, was still full of those who chose to live without using their future-sight gifts. This was beneficial to Mory and his friends because the town had a general consensus that they were just kind travelers from a far-off region of their planet where darker skin tones were more prevalent. Patten still held true to the book of exiles, as with all other previous practices, since the culture of this little, isolated town was exceedingly slow to evolve. The actual book itself had been destroyed in the catastrophe, and it was impossible for anyone to see the images or read the names of the individuals in it anymore. Mory had seen it for himself, or had rather been presented with a pile of ash and paper chunks that the librarian claimed to have been the exile book.

While conversing with the librarian, Mory used his Spirit to piece together some of the books to help her refill the library with the literature that she had thought lost forever. He couldn't piece together ashes, but he could help with the less damaged material. This had helped loosen the lips of the lady a bit more as she couldn't help but be slightly encouraged, even in her grumpy state, by the sight of her life coming back together. There was still another copy of the exile book, a master copy kept by higher-up government, in archives elsewhere on Tendyis. Closton was the name of the location. Mory was glad they had decided to call Scilla by an alias "Lily" since they had entered Tendyis. Better safe than sorry, especially if other copies of her exile status existed.

The repaired steps creaked as he stepped down them and back into the ruins of Patten. The library was the biggest building here and had been made out of the sturdiest materials, so the structure was more intact than the others. A cool dew sprayed on Mory's ankles when he reached the grassy ground which had once been a garden out in front of the library. The constant twilight, broken only by the darkness of night, was proving hard to get used to. It always seemed cool and damp, and then got cooler and damper when the sun set. His skin felt like it might stay a bit prune-like forever. The dim light here was the most difficult thing for him to get used to though. It made it hard for him to see much. He was starting to understand a bit of Scilla's complications living for years on Krael, if this was her normal.

He had to admit, even though it was a little dark for his liking, being able to see the stars during the daytime as well as night was a pleasant experience. The night sky was always so beautiful with the sea of twinkling stars and the rainbow glitter of the galaxy belt on Krael, but most people were asleep during the times that the night's show was the most vivid and spectacular. Here, you could see the exquisite nighttime showing of the stars, or watch their matinee during the day. The dimmer stars were not always visible during the day, the colors were not as vibrant, and their twinkling dance was muted, but the show was still there, going on without pause. It was quite humbling, in Mory's opinion, to be constantly reminded how much more was out there at every moment of the day and night. It made being on a planet full of people who could only see the future on the planet they were on seem simple and mundane. There was so much that they were missing out on seeing. Mory's existence himself was such a small thing in comparison to the greatness of the universe. He would just have to do his best if he wanted to make any sort of ripple through the flow of time and history, and hopefully, his best brought out the best in others along the way.

Mory made a mental note to learn the new patterns in the stars that he was seeing on Tendyis. He realized that not only would it be a fun exercise, but they might be able to use it for location purposes since the stars were always visible.

Mory saw Vi's bright purple light bouncing toward him from far away, a beacon in the constant darkness surrounding her. She approached him blinking her light in an excited cadence, "They like the blapples! They were cautious at first, but now they make an effort to find them."

"Excellent!" Mory responded. Mory, Anik, and Kylie had been leaving blapples around the outskirts of town in hopes to attract the night mares. Combined together, they had packed quite a few of them in their satchels to bring along. They told themselves that having the night mares help with transportation would be beneficial, but if Mory looked deep inside, he knew that he, and likely Kylie and Anik, just missed their pegasi and wished that they were here on

Tendyis with them. The night mares couldn't replace the pegasi, but they could help fill the gap if the group could earn their trust.

Since Vi could see them in her invisible state, she had been watching the night mares and mimicking Scilla's song. She had noticed that the night mares had all flicked their ears toward Scilla's humming the other day, and some had even stopped grazing and turned their heads to listen, so Vi did her best to perfect the tune and entice the creatures to enjoy the blapple treats. Mory realized that they should probably let Scilla in on their plans soon, but she seemed very distracted by so many other things, and capturing the hearts of night mares seemed like a frivolous thing to bother her with right now.

"Can you show me the night mares?" Mory asked Vi, and she nodded vigorously. She waved for him to follow her across the town. Along the way, Kylie and Anik joined him since they likely knew what Vi was leading them toward.

Mory saw two or three of the night mares a good distance away in the field just outside of town, and pieces of blapple cores were laying haphazardly around, dousing the area with their sweet aroma. Vi turned back to her followers and gave them a shushing motion with her tiny finger to her lips before casting her mirage magic on all of them. Suddenly, the field was full of the timid creatures munching peacefully on the dewy grass. The ones closer to them began to dance away skittishly as they realized they could now be seen by the newcomers. Vi started humming the relaxing tune and although the night mares kept their distance, eyeing them suspiciously, they did not run away.

Mory felt excitement building up inside him as he eyed the night mares, so close, yet so far away. "I think we need to show them that we are kind-hearted. Maybe they like being pet? I'll try to approach one of them alone and gauge their reaction."

Mory crouched over slightly with Vi on his shoulder, leaving Kylie and Anik behind to watch in suspense. He stepped slowly toward the apprehensive creatures talking softly and reassuringly. He could get relatively close, but not close enough to touch, before one would dart back slightly shaking its mane in distrust. He tried the process a few times with similar results before he noticed Kylie waving him back. His current tactic obviously wasn't working, so he made his way back to his friends.

"They don't seem to like it when your cloak billows out," Kylie remarked just as a breeze blew in to prove her point. Mory watched his cloak expand, contract, and contort with the wind and could fathom how the night mares may balk at it. After a moment's thought, Mory removed all of Ghaleon's gifts: his cloak, sword, and shield. They were well made for battle, but not horse-catching. He handed them off to his trusted friends and felt much lighter and more suited to the task at hand.

Once again, Mory began his slow approach to the night mares. He tried joining in the tune that Vi was humming as well. The results weren't immediate, but after a few tries he slowly reached his hand out near the nose of one of the braver creatures. She sniffed the air curiously, slowly turning her head to look him in the eye. On his knees, Mory slowly slid forward until his fingers were within inches of the night mare's nose. He could feel her exhaling breaths and smell the familiar scent of horse hide. He paused there for what seemed like ages closing his eyes and bowing his head before her. Eventually, he felt something tickle his hand. It was the delicate brush of nose whiskers. She lipped at his empty hand with her silky muzzle, as if looking for a treat, and Mory very slowly reached his free hand into his pack and pulled out a blapple. If horses could smile, this one did. She switched her sniffing to Mory's blapple-filled hand and nibbled graciously out of it. Mory started scratching her neck and telling her how good of a girl she was. He had started combing his fingers through her mane when she neighed wildly and began to buck and rear.

Mory's fingers were caught, entwined in her mane, and he felt the pain of them pulling. In a flash decision, he swung his leg up and tried to mount the night mare. He landed on her back only to be bucked and flung around like a rag doll as the frightened animal flailed. She started running in circles doing her best to be rid of her new guest. Mory was just trying to keep the horse and himself from harm, so he hung onto her neck as best as he could while trying to speak calmly. His heart raced and his breath came in bursts, making the "calm" portion of speaking challenging. In the confusing blurs of vision that he had in between chunks of mane in his eyes, he could see small creatures growling and screeching while throwing clumps of dirt at the frightened herd. Too much of his mind was occupied with trying to remedy his current situation to try and think about what this all meant.

He heard Kylie and Anik's voices in the chaos, but he couldn't hear what they were saying. He thought he saw them chasing him. Suddenly, the ground rose ahead of him, and the night mare took a sharp left to avoid it. Another ground spike grew. Another sharp left to avoid. This carried on for what seemed like an eternity, one ground spike at a time, and just when Mory thought he couldn't hold on any longer, the night mare slowed to a stop.

He heard soothing lute music cutting through the cacophony of the situation. It was a balm on his feelings as much as the horse's. Eventually, Mory saw that the ground had risen up around them into a small fence-like enclosure. That had to have been Anik. The lute music came none other than from the boy's lute he had mended in the town. After catching his breath on the night mare's back, he slid down her now sweat-logged coat to the ground. She was breathing just as heavily as Mory was, and for a second, they leaned on each other, almost as if keeping each other standing upright. She looked at him at first with fear in her eyes, then they seemed almost apologetic. She finally nuzzled Mory affectionately and butted her head against his shoulder.

Mory looked around and saw Anik, Kylie, and the lute player standing as still and silent as possible, with the exception of the music, outside the corral of ground. When Mory looked each of them in the eye and smiled, they all let out a large breath of relief. Mory walked to the edge of the fence and hopped over. Kylie hugged him immediately upon landing, "I'm so glad you're okay!" He hugged her back just as strongly.

Vi jumped out of the satchel that she had been hiding in and exasperatingly said, "Whew, even inside the bag with near unlimited space, that was shaking!"

Mory shook his head at her, "Why didn't you just fly away?!"

"Well, I wasn't going to leave you to that disaster. We've been through far worse than a bad horse ride!" Vi rolled her eyes at him for not coming to this obvious conclusion sooner.

Anik lowered a section of the wall that he had made back to ground level to let the night mare loose back into the field, but after she looked around the area and saw that her herd had gone elsewhere, she chose to stay near the humans and visible to them as well.

The lute player started explaining as though he felt the need to since the others were outsiders to the town, "Those were groundlings. They have weak to moderate levels of magic that they can use to manipulate the ground." He stamped his foot on the grass to emphasize 'the ground.' "They gather in tribes but usually keep to themselves unless provoked. It is very uncharacteristic of them to aggravate a group of night mares and people. Night mares are soothed by music, and they feed on the fear of others, replacing it with calm. I think that is why she has taken more of a liking to you now. She has been snacking on your recent fear."

Mory did notice that he felt significantly calmer now than he had immediately after his wild ride. He wondered what tasted sweeter to a night mare, fear or blapples.

"Usually once a specific night mare takes a liking to your kind of fear or terror or troubled memories, they will stay near you, or come back to you to continue their snacking. So, I think you've made a new friend, Mory."

Mory looked back at the now content-looking night mare, and she nodded her head at him before reaching down to pull some grass out with her teeth. He looked back to the boy, and apologized, "I'm sorry, I realized I never asked for your name before."

"They call me Lohee. No need for apologies. You fixed my lute up right nice and pretty. It looks even fresher than the day my grandfather gave it to me." Lohee stopped playing his song to admire his lute once more with an involuntary smile creeping across his lips. He stroked it reverently before continuing, "With the magic it now possesses, I'm sure Patten will be back together in no time."

Mory was beaming with the hope that had been imbued into the boy. When he had interacted with him before, Lohee had seemed determined and strong, but melancholy. Now his hope shined bright. Mory wondered if the boy didn't have some sort of magic of his own to which he was unwitting. Mory had never been so moved and seen images so clearly from a piece of music before he heard Lohee play.

"Uh oh." Anik's worried tone drew Mory's attention, and he looked back to see Anik frantically looking in circles on the ground and then looking up into the branches of a nearby tree.

"What is it?" Mory asked.

"Um… well, here is your sword," Anik handed him the weapon, "There is your shield," Anik pointed to the ground a couple of feet away, "But, I don't see your cloak anywhere."

"What happened to it?" Mory cried incredulously. "I left them with you guys when I went to court the night mares!"

Anik explained, "Yes, and we dropped them to come chase your mount after the rodeo began. They were all in a pile right here. I don't know what could have happened to it. I placed the cloak under the shield specifically in case there was a strong breeze that could blow it away."

"The groundlings," Kylie said in a low voice. "Lohee said that it isn't normal for them to act as they did. What if they were put up to this thievery? What if they are similar to the firelings on Krael and susceptible to bribery? There were definitely similarities in their appearances and behaviors, and their harrying of the night mares did seem to stop randomly. They likely were distracting us to grab the cloak."

Mory nodded, "That does seem like a possibility, and we know who would be interested in the cloak and who has experience with this sort of plotting."

Simultaneously, Mory, Kylie, and Anik all said, "Kaitzen."

Mory asked no one in particular, "Did you see which way they ran?"

Kylie answered immediately, "Yes. They ran north of the field and into the forest back there before disappearing from sight. There were maybe about 50 of them. If they are anything like firelings, we could probably put up a good fight in the woods and get your cloak back." Kylie unsheathed her dagger from her cuff, catching enough of the dim light to glint menacingly.

"Be careful if you go there," Lohee warned, "That forest is known as Bellis, the neon forest. It is a beautiful sight to behold, but it is rumored to be haunted by the spirits of those who perished in the battle that was fought here long ago. Strange things happen in Bellis. Some go in and never return. Some come back but are changed mentally or physically to the point of being a ghost of what they were when they entered the tree line. Some babble endlessly, some are forever silent, some quiver constantly with huge, terrified eyes. It's never good."

"Well, that sounds like just the place I would want to chase the groundlings into." Mory said sarcastically, "I'm sure Kaitzen was hoping we'd be scared off or damaged by the forest in some way too if we went after them." Mory paused to think. If Kaitzen was behind this, they needed to act quickly, or else he could escape to some other planet and wreak havoc, but he also had to consider that they would be stronger with the rest of the group together. If they did cross paths with Kaitzen, they needed Scilla to be there to attempt to reason with him. She would be the only one with a chance to get through to him. If they found him without Scilla, and they were forced to kill him, she would not be very happy. Mory wrestled inside with indecision. Before he came to a conclusion, Kylie decided for him.

"I'll go after them. Stealthily, of course. You guys get the others. I won't be seen. I should hurry though." Then she turned to Lohee, "I will take your warning seriously and be careful. Thank you for letting us know of the danger."

"I'll go too," Mory decided, not wanting to let Kylie go on her own into a haunted forest where she could lose her mind. It was one of the most beautiful things about her. "Anik, Lohee, please find and tell the others what happened. We will try to leave a trail for you if you decide to meet up with us."

Anik nodded and waved at them, "Go, go! You may not have much time to follow them."

"Be very careful!" Lohee emphasized again.

Mory gave the night mare a pat and one more blapple snack before jogging with Kylie toward Bellis. Surprisingly, the night mare started to follow. Mory, with a warm feeling of happiness and achievement in his heart, swung himself up onto the horse, pulling up Kylie behind him. She wrapped her arms around his waist, and they made their way toward the thick and sudden tree line at the edge of the field.

Chapter 10

The dim light of the sun was blocked out by the great gnarl of tree branches that formed the forest canopy as soon as they were a few paces into the wooded area. Despite the dense covering, it was not dark within the trees. Blue and green fluorescent, vine-like plants crawled across the paths and trees creating more light than outside of the forest. The tips of Mory's fingernails were bright white in the light, and when he glanced back at Kylie's big smile, it was glowing white too. The name "neon forest" made some sense to him now. It was cool and damp, and a mist hung in the air that Mory could almost drink. He could see the leaves on the plants shining in the glowing light with slick watery films across their surfaces, and he could feel tiny droplets dripping on his head from the trees above. He shook his head for good measure and watched the droplets fly out of his hair.

The night mare's hooves sunk into the muddy ground making a sucking sound each time she pulled her foot up. The moving was slow, but it gave Mory a chance to look down and examine the trail for footprints. The nice thing about the mud was that there were definitely footprints he could see. The bad thing about the mud was discerning which of the many tracks were the ones that he cared about, especially since he didn't get a good look at the groundlings that attacked them.

Kylie was looking down at the ground too with strands of her golden-green hair sticking to her neck from the messy braid that she must have hastily put it into after mounting the night mare. "How will we ever find the right tracks?" she spoke softly, and Mory agreed with her thoughts. They didn't give up though. They took a few guesses from the creature's sizes of what the tracks could have looked like and followed them through the forest as best as they could.

The deeper they went into the forest, the more eerie it felt. A low fog crept in, swirling on the ground, making the tracks more difficult to follow. Mory could have sworn that he saw something move in the ebb and flow of the fog, or maybe something coalesce and then dissipate in the mists, or maybe it was just his imagination.

"Mory, do you hear that?" Kylie whispered frightenedly over his shoulder.

"Are the stars talking to you again?" Mory responded and got a well-deserved poke in the side for his flippant response.

"No! The moaning and whispers!" Kylie insisted.

Mory refocused his mind on listening, and he did hear them. He couldn't make out what they were saying, but he could feel the fury, fear, anxiety, and melancholy in their tones. They were all talking at once mixed with the breeze, almost blowing by with it. Strangely, he wasn't as scared as he thought he should be. He looked down at the night mare who had a perfectly content look on her face. She must be feeding off their fear and keeping them calm. Mory wondered if she was feeding off the other negative feelings of the mists as well. Most horses would have been incredibly skittish in these conditions, but the night mare kept plodding along relatively unconcerned with her surroundings.

As they went on, the swirls became more tangible, and the moans progressed into audible shrieks and sentences. Faces of soldiers of various races and dress were molded into the fog and mists. Their visages carried all the emotions of war. All the emotions that he had sensed earlier were now visualized. Suddenly, a man with sweat pouring down his face and wind thrashing through his hair came straight for Mory, axe raised, loudly screaming the cry of a man running into the frontline of battle. Mory turned his head, ducked his shoulders, and grimaced as the mists hit him and went straight through with no effect. Mory was thankful that these ghosts were unable to harm them because they were well-armed and seemed well-trained. Sometimes they were fighting each other, or fighting something unseen, but many were moving in the same direction that the night mare kept steadily heading toward.

Mory had tried to redirect the night mare a few times, but she would just shake her head and keep moving the original way. Since he had no other reason to change route now that he had failed at following the groundling's tracks, and he had an inkling that maybe the night mare knew or sensed something that he didn't, he let her go on. She seemed to be protecting them from the worst of the ghostly onslaught, preventing their minds from the madness that had tainted others who had dared enter Bellis unprotected. He hoped that her intentions were good and that she wasn't leading them into a trap.

Up ahead, Mory saw the mists avoiding a hemispherical shaped area, curling into finger-like tendrils grasping greedily at an emptiness. It appeared as though they couldn't enter that space. The ghosts were also throwing themselves against the invisible forcefield which caused them to dissipate back into the particles of fog and mist of their construction.

This is where the night mare decided to stop. She began munching on some nice, thick tufts of grass near the base of one of the trees and refused to take another step. Mory and Kylie slid off of her back and decided to cautiously investigate the strange happenings in the area. Even with the night mare feeding off his negative feelings, Mory could still feel tastes of the anger, fear, frustration, and determination bleeding through. There was something else too. Something that brought back memories of when he had acquired Ghaleon's shield while fighting a soulless dragon.

"Vi, does this *feel* familiar to you?" Vi poked her head out of Mory's satchel where she had been hiding from the ghosts and the chilly, wetness of the forest.

"Yes, it does. I don't like this feeling. I don't know if we can survive another fight like that."

"Kylie is here this time too, and we've had more experience training with the sword and shield now. I don't have the cape, but we didn't have it then either. Plus, isn't this what I'm supposed to be doing as the Spirit Master? Getting rid of evils like this?" Mory responded with words sounding much more confident than he felt.

"I suppose," Vi said, "But I still don't like it." Vi popped the rest of the way out of the satchel and looked to be readying herself for the possibility of an upcoming battle with a determined look on her little face. "You know I'll be here for you. I am at your command!" Vi ran her fingers through her purple hair and did her best with the natural wetness of the air to stick it up in a spiky, menacing manner that Mory was forced to suppress a smile with the seriousness of her actions.

"Thanks, Vi, I'm sure we will get through this together," Mory emphasized before turning to Kylie, who had drawn her cherished knife, Regithal's gift from many years ago, out of her sleeve while he had been conversing with Vi. She was taking stock of the nearby area, peeking around trees, turning over leaves the size of small blankets fallen onto the ground, and periodically kicking rocks at the shield to see what happened to them. Each of them bounced off, unable to penetrate the shield.

He interrupted her investigation, "Kylie, there may be a difficult battle ahead."

She nodded, "I'm ready." She had been listening to his conversation with Vi, and he had told her of what had happened when he found Ghaleon's shield. She knew whatever was beyond the barrier before them could be incredibly dangerous. If she was afraid, she was doing a good job of hiding it, or maybe the night mare had just gobbled up all of it.

Mory looked back at the night mare. She had paused her grass munching for a moment to look into Mory's eyes. He thought she was telling him that she would support him too, but he didn't have any good way to know for sure. He gave her a good neck scrub with his fingers before drawing his sword and confronting the barrier.

With a lack of fear and a strange calm in an otherwise terrifying situation, Mory raised his sword and delicately touched the barrier. He had learned from previous experience that was all it may need to be broken by his powerful sword. The invisible hemispherical forcefield shattered in a grand manner that could only partially be seen as it perturbed the fog and mists while exploding into the forest ceiling. Some pieces even broke through the interwoven branches and escaped into the dim daylight sky.

The ghostly figures crowding the base of the shield were finally able to descend upon what was inside. No longer did they dissipate upon hitting a barrier. They flung themselves in all their battle fury at their common opponent.

Mory saw the dragon-like creature unfurl itself from a sleep-like state on the ground. Its long red neck with thinly curved black spikes, almost bristle-like, uncoiled straight up, and its bright yellow eyes surveyed the area intelligently. Moss and the vine-like glowing substance had grown over its long-stagnant body, pinning it to the ground. Before Mory could take advantage and strike, huge red wings that were also adorned with black bristle-like spikes unfolded, breaking away the years of forest growth that had blanketed the dragon. The undersides of the wings and belly were a slightly lighter red, hinting at an orange, but did not look any less penetrable than the outer red scales. What the wings did not free the dragon of, the curved black claws did, as they ripped the shackles of greenery away with no problems.

The ghostly creatures bombarded the now-standing dragon with its chest pushed out in a deep breath before exhaling a blood-curdling screech, but the ghosts had no physical effect on the dragon. It was looking down on their futile onslaught condescendingly when it saw Mory and his companions. Its eyes lit up, and a toothy grin spread across its maw revealing sharp, yellowing teeth with strands of spittle threading through them like a gooey floss. Mory heard a raspy, deep, harsh voice in his mind, "I hunger. Your souls are mine."

Without any further ado, Mory rushed in with a battalion of ghosts ahead of him and his friends behind him. The dragon raised a massive foreclaw, and as he slashed with it, Mory returned the blow and trimmed his fingernails down to blunt clubs as opposed to razor-sharp swords. This irritated the dragon who started bludgeoning Mory with that same foreclaw, but Ghaleon's shield protected him, and the blows did not seem nearly as hard as they could have been. Mory tried to land another blow, but the dragon was a fast learner and was agile enough to avoid the swings of the sword.

The dragon picked up a boulder in its mouth and threw it in Mory's direction. He pulled the shield up over his head and let the boulder that would have crushed anything else bounce off like a pebble on a tin roof. The wretched smell of its breath that wafted over before the release made Mory a bit woozy. Once the unsteadiness passed, he moved his shield back to his side. The dragon had turned its attention to Kylie who had made her way up its back and was clinging to a bundle of bristle spikes while trying to slash the underside of the dragon's neck. Mory could see that the scales looked to be overlapping, and he knew that's what Kylie was trying to strike. She must think that there was tender flesh beneath the hard scales. The dragon was awkwardly bending its neck down, trying to bite at her, before he started shaking vigorously in an attempt to throw her off.

Mory needed to get the dragon's attention back onto him to give Kylie any chance of succeeding. "Vi, go help, Kylie! Turn her invisible!" Vi obediently flew off in a purple streak, trusting Mory to take care of himself. He had an idea. Drawing on his Spirit, he bid the vines to grow once again, extremely quickly. Green and blue light crawled over the fore and hind claws of the dragon and pinned its tail to the ground. Just as he would rip one limb free, another would become stuck. Its attention was sufficiently off of Kylie now, and Mory saw that she had been successful. An orangish scale of its neck fell, and the thump it made reverberated across the ground. A small piece of the beast's armor was broken. Mory hoped it was enough.

The dragon raised its head and made a few coughing noises from which Mory saw spurts of something frightening puff upwards: smoking, hot fire. Once its throat was cleared, and the fire tubes seemed to be working again, it looked at Mory once more, taking aim.

The vines were creeping up the thighs and biceps of the dragon, but that didn't hinder its fire breath aim with its snake-like neck. When Mory saw the mouth of the beast open while facing his direction, he raised his shield. The fire felt like the pressure of a waterfall plummeting down on him. It got more powerful in strength with time, and he could feel the growing heat seeping through.

Mory had studied the ways of light and recalled how it traveled in waves. He willed those wavelengths to be small enough to weave their way through the metallic shield and into his eyes so he could see what was happening on the other side of the shield barrier. At first, he saw only the red-hot fire, but he shifted slightly so he could see the body of the dragon. There. He saw it now. The chink in the beast's armor that Kylie had made. He angled the shield until the fire stream bounced back onto the dragon. Initially, its armor protected it, but when Mory aimed just right, he hit the bare skin of the dragon, and the pain was unbearable for the beast.

It stopped shooting the fire once it realized how it was hurting itself. Mory took the opportunity given to him and ran up the body of the dragon rapidly being tangled in the vines. He used his Spirit to enhance his climbing and jumping abilities, scaling the vines and the dragon with speed and precision, racing the constantly growing vegetation to his ultimate goal.

Just before the vines reached the bared spot on the dragon's neck, Mory sunk his sword into the flesh of the dragon, and in a shriek of pain, the vile creature disappeared. Mory fell for a while before landing in a relatively soft, and somewhat wet, pile of vegetation that had once been engulfing his foe. He stared up into the treetops while he caught his breath. He was exhausted from the battle, but he had never felt his soul being ripped from his body, so he counted himself lucky. He figured that he had the night mare to thank for that boon with her unique magic.

He dragged himself up into a sitting position and surveyed the area. The charging ghosts were dissolving one by one into the mists and fog, decreasing the density of the charge upon the area where the dragon once stood, where Mory lay now. The facial expressions of the ghosts seemed to be more relaxed as they disappeared. Some had even dropped their weapons or at least held them in a relaxed state instead of battle ready. Some held their arms open while staring up into the sky, others fell to the ground, finally resting.

The leaves and vines next to him crunched down suddenly, startling Mory. Was this a ghost? Mory stared wide-eyed into the emptiness beside him waiting for *something* to happen when Kylie appeared with Vi, who was laughing hysterically. "Vi, there are better times for joking around!" Mory scolded her while clasping at his chest.

"Are there really, though? We all seemed to need a little pick-me-up after that battle," she replied before continuing her jovial laughter. Kylie seemed to have found the joke amusing as well. She wasn't laughing as hard, but she had a smile on her face.

"I advised her against it for what it's worth, but saw no real harm in her prank, so I complied," Kylie explained to him with a slight shrug of her shoulders.

"It's okay. You guys just gave me a start," Mory said while glancing over at the night mare. Shouldn't her magic have kept his startled reaction away? Maybe somehow there was a difference between true fear and friendly fear, or maybe she was also in on the prank. He thought he saw her wink one of her ice-blue eyes at him. Yeah, he figured that was the case. He was surrounded by too many girls at the moment.

Mory pulled himself off the ground and noticed the black blood of the dragon was similar to that of the one he had battled before when he found the shield of Ghaleon on Krael. They must have been similar kinds of creatures. The black blood singed the forest ground wherever it touched, but his blade and clothing seemed unperturbed by it. He wondered if there was something special about this ground that did not mix with the blood.

He walked back to the night mare and began to look around once more for any tracks, encouraging Kylie and Vi to do the same. The ghosts didn't seem to leave any tracks, but there must have been a thriving number of other creatures in the forest to sculpt the ground as it was. The night mare let out a loud whinny and slowly the forest wildlife began to emerge. First, a flight of beautiful butterflies with shiny fluorescent wings dotted the wooded area. A rainbow of colors danced around him. Then tiny rodents with two tails and two long floppy ears began peeking out from holes in the ground. Each of their tails was tipped with neon. The deer-like creatures were next with three horizontal neon stripes down their backs. All the creatures of the neon forest seemed to have some sort of light branded on their skins or fur. How could he not see them before!? They were masters of camouflage. A fuzzy creature with human-like hands and a flat face pulled back some bushes, followed by others. Tall stones carved with ancient words were revealed from behind the bushes. Gravestones. Mory finally realized that they stood on a graveyard. Maybe that was why the dragon's blood burned. It was contacting the hallowed ground.

Mory knelt down in reverence, bowing his head in silence. The ghosts that had bombarded the dragon were likely from this graveyard he supposed, and he wanted to pay them respect for the battle that they had been waging for who knows how long. Kylie followed his gesture. The night mare trotted over to the nearest stone and placed some flowers on it that she had picked from nearby, folding one of her front legs in to kneel as well as a horse could.

After they all had paid respects, another creature appeared from the forest. It was a horse-sized lizard, or maybe a small dragon. Regardless, it seemed friendly and carried itself in a regal manner. The horned bones on his head were shaped into a natural crown, his skin was a mottled coloring of scales, and he held a large walking stick in one clawed hand with a carved eagle adorning its top. "Thank you, my friends, for restoring the peace to Bellis. As recompense, I will show you the way to the groundling's home, which I have seen your desire, and also the way out of the woods." He paused and looked each of them in the eyes before continuing, "I bid you to remember in your hearts that the groundlings, although easily manipulated, are still one of the forest kin."

Mory nodded and understood what the forest king was telling them. They shouldn't kill the groundlings unless necessary. The small dragon waved his stick, and flowers opened up in yellow and red pathways. "Any way you go, the flowers will open red to lead you to the groundlings' home and yellow to take you back to the location from which you entered the forest. Once you leave the forest, the enchantment will retire," the forest king explained.

He turned around and began to melt back into the wooded area, "Go now in peace, as that is the gift you have given to us as well. The forcefield you dispelled was made of the remnants of the souls of the soldiers that you used to see in this forest. Now that they no longer have to maintain that shield, and now that the rest of their souls have been released from the beast that you have slain, they have departed to rest in the afterlife. A rest they have long awaited and deserve."

"Wait!" Mory called, "We never learned your name!"

"My name matters not, I will know when you call for me if you are within the forest," the forest king said as he disappeared entirely from view into the fern-fringed shadows, tail sweeping a few leaves off the path before he was gone. Mory had a sense that if he walked in that direction, he would not find the forest king again. He didn't seem the type that would show himself unless it was his desire.

Kylie and Mory mounted the night mare once more, and with an enthusiastic Vi flying beside them, they followed the red-flowered path watching in awe as the flowers winked back into their original colors after they passed by.

***

Ghaleon looked down at the mortal world with mixed emotions. He was proud that Mory had been able to take down another one of the aberrations born from the latent evil within the hearts of the living. He was also grateful that it had been destroyed before it evolved into a full-fledged splicer, but he felt ashamed, once more, at his past stubbornness toward the Greatest Spirit. He hoped that he could apologize one day, or that the Greatest Spirit could sense his feelings now.

Battlefields were a common place for heroics, but also an area where evil could easily be born. This battlefield that spanned the forest and beyond, behind the town of Patten, had been a particularly brutal one. The number of betrayals that had occurred, neared the number of selfless heroics. These beast-like aberrations grew in strength as they absorbed the souls of those around them and fed off the evil that they found in the hearts of living things until they could morph into larger more capable beings. The spirits who had passed in this battle had found a way to hold back some of the pure good in their souls and use that to trap the evil beast until he could be slain.

Ghaleon had felt the wave of souls enter the realm of rest and understood their contentment at returning to their loved ones once more. Usually, waves of distress and sadness accompanied mass traversals like this one, but this was a unique case. Those souls had earned their rest. If that beast had not been contained and prevented from feeding, who knows what awful deeds it could have accomplished across the universe.

Chapter 11

Kylie couldn't hear the stars as clearly in the forest as she had in Patten. This past night, beneath the trees, the calling of the stars had been more muffled than even on Krael. It was like being used to falling asleep to the sound of crickets chirping, and then one night the crickets were silent. Ever since arriving on Tendyis, she could hear the stars speak to her during the day and night. It made some sort of sense considering the stars were now visible during both timeframes, but it was a noticeable change from Krael.

She couldn't always understand everything that they were saying, but it always sounded encouraging, if not a bit mysterious. The common theme seemed to be them wanting her to let the light into her heart and to share its strength with others. She felt as though she had been letting in their light when she opened herself to their calling, but she hadn't quite been able to share it with others yet. She had tried willing it to others, like she had done naturally with her Spirit, but that didn't seem to yield any effect. She had tried physically touching someone she intended to share it with without success as well. She hoped the stars would speak more clearly to her on that aspect soon.

They had been following the red flowers for a while this morning, and there looked to be a clearing up ahead. Kylie thought she could hear an odd chaos breaking through the forest harmony coming from the clearing. Jovial chanting and shrieking, and maybe some grunting that almost sounded melodious. Could something be singing? Mory slid off the night mare's back, turned to Kylie, and put his finger to his mouth to indicate that she should remain silent. After a short pause, he waved for her to follow him. Kylie followed.

They snuck behind some large fronded plants, and each parted a leaf to the side to peek through. What they saw was not quite what they had been expecting. Small, dark grey, rough-skinned creatures with horns that glowed neon colors were dancing in a circle around a bonfire in the center of a clearing surrounded by tree houses. They almost looked a little goofy with their oversized triangle ears coming nearly horizontal out of their heads and their spindly arms waving around to the beat of the music. Some of the creatures had floral necklaces that almost draped down to their knees, while others held fluffy green fronds in each hand waving them synchronously in a particular pattern.

The song that they were singing was deepened by their voices, and Kylie could feel the rumbling in her chest from the low notes in their rhythmic chanting. Portions of the song were highlighted with almost joyous-sounding shrieking. Kylie thought how interesting it would have been to understand their language enabling her to follow along with the song, but she could feel from the music that it was celebratory in nature.

Beyond the bonfire, there were vine ladders hanging down from the trees giving access to the dwellings overhead. The tree houses were made of wood and neon plants that blended well into the local treescape. Glowing vine bridges snaked across the air connecting various houses with pathways. The dwellings' doors seemed to be mostly vegetation woven together into curtains that parted for those who traversed their boundaries.

Along with the dancing around the bonfire, there were smaller groundlings bouncing on a patch of large mushroom tops as a group. They were weaving back and forth with each other in hops across the mushrooms, giggling in a mischievous way. Other groundings, larger than the bouncers, but smaller than the bonfire dancers, were sneaking about and pulling berries and meat off of a large table while the others were occupied. There seemed to be a joy amongst the groundling clan that they had found.

"These are the beasts that attacked us and stole your cloak?" Kylie whispered to Mory. "That doesn't seem in character compared to what we see here, and I know I would have remembered neon glowing horns if I had seen them outside the forest…unless some things only glow inside the forest."

Mory nodded his agreeance, pointing to their now glowing teeth, but maintained his silence. He was looking for something. Probably something to tell him where his cloak was hiding. Mory's head snapped suddenly in a direction near the dwellings, and then he was swiftly and silently moving his way toward it. Kylie recognized that he must have been using his Spirit to silence the sounds his footfalls made upon the rustling vegetation and squishy mud, and she attempted to mimic the effect on her own so she could follow.

They skirted the edge of the camp, and Mory started scaling a ladder up to the dwellings as far away from the bonfire festivities as possible. Kylie scrambled up quickly after him and pulled herself onto the wooden platform atop the ladder trying her best to keep her eye on Mory's movement as well as the locations of any groundlings who may not have been at the bonfire. The planks of wood on the platforms of the dwellings would have no doubt made creaking noises from their footsteps had they not been muffled. As Kylie stood, she grasped the vine railing nearest her for balance since the entirety of the structure seemed to be moving with the wind.

She caught a glimpse of what Mory must have been following. Someone or something just vanished into a dwelling across a nearby vine bridge. That dwelling was larger than most of the others and had totem poles with stacked creatures carved of wood outlining its perimeter. Mory was already crossing the swaying bridge as carefully and quickly as possible toward the dwelling's door. Kylie did a quick scan for alternate routes and found that if she crossed two bridges in a different direction, then she could come around the backside of that large hut, possibly enabling her to cut off whatever they were pursuing.

Kylie took that path, as leery as the bridges made her, and circled behind the hut just in time to see a tall male with a short bow strapped to his back with his thick, chocolate brown hair loose in the wind as he leaped off the wooden platforms onto the back of a large, magnificent white bird with neon streaks along the feather veins of its wings. As he had leaped, Kylie had thrown one of her smaller throwing daggers and caught a corner of his cloak. A piece of the cloth had ripped free and stuck to the wooden dwelling pinned by her dagger. This was as she intended. She hadn't wanted to hurt the man since she didn't know his purpose, but she wanted to have some way to track him down in case he was important. She saw Mory's head poke up into the window that the man must have escaped out from, and they both watched him fly away astride his white bird weaving elegantly through the tangle of trees.

"He has Ghaleon's cloak," Mory spoke to her dejectedly hanging his head through the window over his crossed arms. "This must be the chief's hut, and it was locked inside a trunk in here that had a mirror on top of it. That man had the key already. He unlocked it, pulled the cloak out, ignored everything else, and then made off with it! I don't think he saw us following him, but maybe he did since he made that quick escape."

Kylie pulled her dagger out of the side of the hut and showed Mory the piece of cloth that she had ripped from him. "At least we have this!" She held up the swatch and let it wave in the wind a bit for him to see.

"You're brilliant, Kylie! Hopefully, we can use this to find him and figure out what he wants with that cloak. He didn't fit the description of Kaitzen, so he must be another Tendyian who somehow got word of this."

"The future sight," Kylie stated pensively. "I wonder how many people do know of this since almost everyone on this planet can see the future."

"But so quickly? And we've been trying to block people's ability to sense our futures with mind walls as well. Scilla said it was difficult for people who can even see the future to foresee specific things that are outside of what they are consciously looking for. I can't believe many were looking for Ghaleon's cloak or anything related to Kaitzen or Scilla. Scilla's visions that randomly overtake her are rare even for Tendyians. They can show seers events that will more assuredly happen, even if they are not along the paths the seer usually chooses to walk of the future, but the prophecies generated by those random occurrences are almost always encrypted in riddles and images, unlike the forced instances. Sometimes the random occurrences are even visions of the past." Mory seemed a bit flustered as he spoke.

Kylie shrugged, "It's the first thing that I can think of, and it sort of makes sense. We should try to follow him before things get more complicated. Our goal is to get your cloak, after all." Kylie heard something. Groundlings were coming across the bridges. "Move Mory! Some groundlings are coming! Let's get back to the night mare and think about how best to follow our mystery man."

Mory climbed through the open window, and both of them leaped off the dwelling's platforms into the trees, grabbing vines and swinging deftly passed the trunks while sliding downward. They both made it back to the night mare's side who was merrily munching on mushrooms. The same mushrooms that the small groundlings had been bouncing on.

One of the young groundlings had left the main group and had found the night mare hidden back in the woods. It had begun stroking her mane and cooing to her. She seemed unperturbed by this, but Mory and Kylie were hesitant to come out into sight while it was there. The night mare made their decision for them. She locked eyes with Mory, and the groundling looked with interest in their direction. The night mare whinnied softly, almost encouraging them to come out of hiding. The curious groundling child walked over and peered into the bushes that Kylie and Mory were hidden in. He peeled back the leaves a little below the level of Kylie's face while she was crouching down, "Um…hi?" she said in the tongue of the people of Patten as the groundling jumped back in surprise.

The groundling didn't run away. It just looked more excited, clapped its hands, and then came back to take another look in the bushes. This time, speaking as best as it could in the same language Kylie had used, "It okay. Nico no hurt. Nico nice. Come play with Nico?" Mory and Kylie emerged from the bushes together and looked down at Nico. He came no higher than their calves, and his ears seemed to be even more disproportioned to his body than the adults around the bonfire. His horns were just tiny knobs barely peeking out from his skull. He must have been an adolescent groundling. Nico wrung his hands together and his eyes shone with excitement. "Nico pet? Nico show friends he is nice." With those words Nico reached out his grey, three-fingered hand and touched Kylie's ankle softly, gently petting it.

"See Nico nice. Nico no hurt you," Nico was smiling and clearly proud of himself for his set of new forest friends.

"You won't tell any of the other groundlings that we are here will you, Nico?" Kylie asked.

"No! Of course not! You are Nico's secret friends. Other groundlings not like Nico much. Nico different. Do you like Nico?

"Of course!" Kylie exclaimed. "You have been so kind to us!" Nico beamed at Kylie's praise. He ran back to the night mare and brought back some berries that they had seen on the table near the bonfire.

"Friends want snack? Nico share his snack!" Nico excitedly put his hands out, offering them the berries.

"No, thank you, Nico, we are in a bit of a hurry to find someone," Nico's shoulders fell as well as his floppy ears at Kylie's response.

"You no stay long with Nico then," he said dejectedly, then his ears perked back up again. "Maybe you take Nico with you! Nico can help you on journey to find someone! Nico know woods around here. Know where to find food and best shelter trees. Please, Nico no want to stay with mean kids anymore. Nico tired of getting made fun of. Nico wants to go on adventure with friends."

Nico was now on his knees hugging Kylie's ankle that he had been petting previously while he fervently begged. Vi popped out of Mory's satchel. "Nico can ride with me in here. There's plenty of room in a nearly endless sack. Sounds like he could have some good information for us too."

Mory nodded and with that, their crew grew by one. The night mare seemed to agree with the decision as she nodded her head before continuing to munch her mushrooms.

Mory asked their new recruit, "Well, Nico, have you ever seen a tall man with rich brown hair around these parts before? He carries a short bow and flies on a large, white bird with neon streaks in it feathers."

Nico gasped in response, "Miran, the hunter!" His ears perked up, grey eyes widened, and hands covered his mouth in surprise.

"So, you've seen him?" Mory asked.

"Seen, no. Heard of, yes. Miran great hunter of exiled. On Tendyis, it common practice to exile different ones or criminals. Tradition span all races. Plane of Portals nearby to dispose of exiled. Others of tribe say Nico will be exiled soon, if Nico not change. Nico lucky he young. Nico scared. If exile return from disposal, Miran will hunt down. Miran come from long line of hunters. Miran never miss mark."

"I see," Mory said. "And do you know where this fabled Miran lives?"

"Nico know the stories! Nico show you! Miran live in neon forest in stories." Nico was pulling at his ears in excitement knowing that he may be of help to his new friends. His little webbed feet, perfect for shoveling dirt, were prancing up and down in place, eager to move toward their destination.

"Well then, let's get a move on! We saw him recently and have a piece of his cloak," Mory gestured to the cloth in Kylie's hand. "He has something of mine that I need to get back."

Kylie knelt down and let Nico examine the piece of cloak. "Nico smell scent on cloak. Nico remember smell and help match later for you. Nico has good nose."

"Thank you, Nico," Kylie said, and she scooped him up in her hands as she stood, placing him inside Mory's satchel. He peeped his head out next to Vi, and they both looked excited to continue on their adventure.

Kylie turned to Mory, "Hunter of exiles? What about Scilla?"

Mory put his hand on her shoulder, "I thought the same thing too. We need to get back to her and warn her if she hasn't seen him in her visions. She is likely safe for now. If Miran has Ghaleon's cloak, I'm pretty sure the one he is currently after is Kaitzen. I have a hunch that he is using the cloak as bait to lure Kaitzen to him. With any luck, we can find both the cloak and Kaitzen when we find Miran."

Chapter 12

Earlier that morning...

Miran, known to many as "the watcher" and "the hunter," sat shirtless and cross-legged on his overly large, silky, meditation pillow, as he did every morning. The scent of his sweetly fragrant tea on the short table to his side filled the room with a relaxing aroma when blending with the woody smell of the forest outside. The glow of the forest plants shone down on him from the nearby window as he breathed in a deep calming breath. His eyes were closed, allowing for better concentration on the possible paths of the future that he was walking.

He walked those paths every morning. His duty was to protect Tendyis from returning exiles, and so every morning he searched. Every afternoon he trained. Every evening he researched. Some would have felt his solitary life monotonous, but Miran used the routine to hone his abilities beyond those of many mortals on Tendyis. He could not allow himself to be bested by anything if he was expected to purge exiles. Returning exiles came from other planets. He knew not what he could be pitted against, so he trained endlessly.

It was not often that an exile found their way back to Tendyis. As a matter of fact, Miran had never had to hunt one as long as he lived. His father had told him about his hunts, and Miran had studied his records thoroughly and religiously. This made training a little tricky, and the afternoons that he did not spend on his own training ground, he spent hunting down trouble-making beasts and runaway criminals. Criminals who were generally running away to avoid exile. Miran tried to convince himself that those criminal encounters counted partially toward his duty fulfillment.

He had been successful in all previously assigned tasks. Not that anyone assigned anything to Miran. He merely followed his own sense of duty. Those looking for help with local beasts or criminals would leave their requests in writing within a box that Miran had created outside the neon forest. No one wanted to enter the haunted neon forest, and this was a large reason why he chose to take up residence here. He had found earlier in his life that visitors were usually annoying and took away from his time dedicated to watching, training, and researching. His only companion, Lucy, one of the last remaining dewls of her kind, would fly out periodically to check his request box for him.

Miran had found Lucy's egg while eradicating a large basilisk from Blain Mountain at the request of some simple mountain townsfolk. The basilisk had killed her parents and eaten her unhatched siblings. Luck had it that day, that Miran engaged the beast before it finished off Lucy's egg. When the basilisk fell from its fight with Miran, its weight shook the tree where Lucy's nest resided, and her egg fell on top of Miran. Miran took pity on the last, lonely egg and took it home with him to care for. Lucy had been loyally by Miran's side ever since.

Lucy's large beak appeared outside through the nearby window, dropping the latest mail into the basket on the floor inside. She was too big to be inside the hut anymore, so she roosted in the trees above and peeked in on occasion when Miran was inside. This meant Miran spent a good deal of his time outside sharing in the company of the great bird, which he didn't mind. Dewls were eagle-like birds massive enough for a full-sized human to ride into the sky. Though as far as

Miran knew, he was the only living being to have flown upon one and survived to tell the tale.

Lucy turned her head so her huge hazel eye could see in through the window and squawked a polite good morning before going to eat her breakfast that she had caught along the way back. She got along quite well in the forest for a mountain bird.

Miran sighed as he saw his request basket was brimming. It was fuller than it had ever been. Usually, he took care of requests immediately, not allowing for any pile-up. At this accumulation rate, he may need a new basket soon. He had to put his exile hunting duties first before tending to the needs of the rest of the nation, but something still nagged at him for not answering those letters. They were the very things that had given him purpose in all the years he had waited for an exile to return to Krael, and those people needed help too. But an exile had indeed returned, Kaitzen. He was an exile from the small town of Patten who had been sent to the Plane of Portals as a young child for killing his father. He was proving to be very slippery to find, and Miran needed to put all his efforts into locating and capturing him.

He had been thrown a recent twist that was threatening to perturb his natural state of cool-headed calmness. Scilla, Kaitzen's twin sister, had also returned from her exile. In all his life not a single exile, and now his first true test would be two at once. He had never failed a mission he had taken before, and he would not let himself fail this time. Miran was confident and sure of his abilities; he just needed to execute.

He had decided to leave Scilla alone, for now, unless an opportunity arose, since his study of her future was oddly hazy and somewhat blocked from him. It had been that way since her arrival. Her paths of the future that he did see, all seemed to have positive impacts on Tendyis. Once Scilla had arrived in his visions, Miran's visions of Kaitzen soon after got similarly hazy and blocked. Whereas Scilla's impact on Tendyis seemed to be helpful, Kaitzen's had a fair amount of destruction and negativity associated with him. He had already caused enough mayhem in Patten to shame Miran for his lack of instantaneous action. Kaitzen needed to be hunted. For his past crimes as well as his probable future ones too. Miran would protect Tendyis, and his father would be proud.

Miran put on one of his tan leather vests, threw his bow and quiver over his shoulder, and went outside to his training yard. He found shooting arrows at his tree targets peaceful, and it helped him to think and practice simultaneously. Miran craved efficiencies and strove to implement them every time a chance was presented to him. On his way to the targets, he walked by Lucy and gave her soft feathers a good ruffle and stroke. Lucy cooed and paused her breakfast to nuzzle Miran with the smooth cheek of her face, careful to keep the dripping blood from her fresh carcass away from Miran's clothing. She knew that blood-stained. She was no stranger to its effects with her meticulous preening to keep her snow-white feathers pristinely clean.

Once Lucy turned back to her meal, Miran pulled out his first arrow and took aim, letting his mind wander as his shots hit the bullseye with nothing but consistency. Kaitzen had been thwarting Miran for too long now. It was embarrassing and blemishing his reputation. Kaitzen had perfected acting without planning and never stayed in one place very long, making it difficult for Miran to capture him. With Scilla's return, his possible future paths changed drastically. Not for the better, but drastically, nonetheless. Kaitzen craved something more than revenge now, and Miran would be sure to get his hands on that cloak that he wanted so badly, whatever it exactly was, before Kaitzen ever could see it beyond a vision. That cloak contained powers that Miran did not want in Kaitzen's hands, and with any luck, after it had served his purpose, Miran would return the cloak to its rightful owner who had also arrived on Tendyis with Scilla.

Part of his conscious warned him about returning something with that immense power to an acquaintance of an exile, but another part assured him it was the right thing to do, eventually. Even if "eventually" meant after dealing with Scilla too. After all, he was a hunter of exiles, not a hunter of those alien to Tendyis. So long as those aliens meant no harm to his home, he had nothing to hold against them.

Scilla was another issue entirely. In the short time since she had returned, she had brought the renewal of hope to the town that Kaitzen had destroyed and had not caused any trouble. All her futures led to positive endings, even if there were struggles along the journey. Could she have changed from the father murderer that she was when she was exiled? Could it be that the ancestors of those of Patten had wrongly accused her? It was possible.

The people of Tendyis could not walk the paths of the past at will. Those blessed, or cursed, with sudden visions had been known to have visions of the past strike them rarely, but not a single Tendyian had been known to purposefully walk the times of the past. Once a crime had been committed, or once any moment had passed, or had merely become the present, those doors were closed to the seers. They knew all of what could be, but none of what actually happened. And worse, those of Patten refused to walk even the paths of the future because of their culture. They lived blind. It was possible that they could have exiled people without checking their possible future paths. They could have wrongly accused a good and kind Tendyian, issuing out the ultimate punishment to an innocent life: exile.

But then again, there was something odd about Scilla, the way his visions slipped around her and her companions like water slipping through his fingers as he tried to grasp it. Sometimes they were wholly blocked from him. Maybe she could somehow alter his visions into showing him a positive future when she really meant ill? But Kaitzen's visions had started acting in the same mysterious manner, and his still showed nothing but evil. Miran was confusing himself now, overthinking the many possibilities. A problem that many seers exhibited.

In order to stay focused on Kaitzen, Miran would have to drop his thoughts on Scilla. He was a sworn hunter of exiles. That was his duty. Nothing in there mentioned if they were guilty or not, just if they were exiles, then they were to be hunted and removed by any means necessary. He would have to examine that moral conundrum more closely when he had the mind and time for it. For now, Scilla would wait.

When he was finished with his target practice, Miran went to go grab the arrows from the spiral shape that he had created on the target expanding out from the bullseye. All the arrows were still within the bullseye circle, just in slightly different locations. He had taken to doing this long ago, so as not to split his arrows from hitting the center of the bullseye repeatedly. It was not efficient for him to keep making new arrows, and making an intentional spiral shape was just as good as hitting the bullseye in his opinion.

It was nearing time for him to visit the groundling camp. He walked over to his pond and knelt down to cleanse the sweat from his brow. The waters of the neon forest were beautiful, even in mere ponds or puddles. If Miran looked closely, he could see shimmers of color within the water. Particularly, when he ran his hand through it and watched the colors swirl around it, sometimes sparkling, beneath the surface. Those were the minerals and micro-organisms that provided nourishment and cleanliness to the water. Miran knew the colors well enough to be able to discern whether a body of water was drinkable, or not, solely based upon the shimmering colors beneath the water's surface. It was a useful skill for a man of the wilderness to know. This particular pond was one of the most pristine he had seen and was a large part of his decision to make his home here.

It was odd, he knew the exact time that he would have to leave in order to give him the best chance of success at obtaining the cloak, but his success wasn't a given. He would still have to try his hardest and follow his plans to a tee. If all panned out, not only would he leave the groundling camp unnoticed by the groundlings, humble forest beings with limited mental capacity, but he *would* be seen by the owner of the cloak. He felt a pang of guilt knowing that if he chose not to intervene today that the most likely path of the future had been a success on behalf of the cloak's owner, but there had always been a chance of the boy's failure and the possibility that the cloak would have fallen into Kaitzen's grubby hands. Miran could not let that happen, and he could not let a chance slide away to grab something so desired by Kaitzen that he may actually come to Miran to retrieve it. This was Miran's best chance at honoring his duty, and he was going to take it.

Chapter 13

Bellis forest felt comforting and familiar to Scilla as she strolled through its neon-dotted foliage with her companions closely following. She had visited here many times as a child accompanied by her night mare friend to escape the mundanity of her everyday life. The forest seemed more settled now than it had so many years ago. She hadn't seen a single ghost yet. When she was young, she had become accustomed to seeing glimpses of them darting through the trees and sneaking through the ferns. She had even once followed them toward an area where many of them seemed to congregate. From the warning that Lohee had given them a day ago when Kylie and Mory had gone chasing after Ghaleon's stolen cloak, Scilla had expected the forest to still be haunted by ghosts from the ancient war, but deep within herself, Scilla sensed a change in this place. It was peaceful. The unrest and eeriness that her old night mare friend had protected her from so long ago were gone.

Yesterday evening, as Scilla, Anik, Dainn, and Elasche were preparing and provisioning to go searching for their friends frolicking in the forest, they had seen a strange purplish-blue glow transcending above Bellis and into the star-filled heavens. It had not lasted very long, but it lit up the sky enough that Scilla and the other Tendyians in Patten had to squint in order not to be blinded by the sudden burst of light. Scilla suspected that Mory and Kylie were behind the light show and that its appearance must be linked to the purging of the haunts inside the neon forest. Scilla was proud of those two. She may have been hard on them when they were growing up while studying in the Ancient Archives, but she felt like it had made them stronger and better prepared for the onerous lives that they were forced to lead.

Scilla's purpose in Bellis was two-fold. The first part was to reunite with Kylie and Mory, providing them with any aid that they needed in retrieving Ghaleon's cloak. That was their guaranteed safe passage back to Krael. Contrary to the others in her party, she was not quite as worried about the dynamic duo. She had walked the paths of the future and had found that they would likely be okay. She knew that this was not absolutely certain on a planet full of seers constantly tweaking the future, but she also knew how capable Kylie and Mory were. Regardless, she would not leave them alone for long. She especially wanted to get back to them before they had any chance of encountering Kaitzen. Scilla didn't want to chance any harm coming to Kaitzen before she had a chance to try and reach the brother she had grown up with. She had to at least try.

The second part of her purpose in Bellis was to locate a clarum deposit in a reachable area so that she could harvest some charged specimens to take back with her to Krael. She wanted to maintain her future-sight capabilities there if she could. The librarian in Patten had mentioned a promising place in the forest that may allow her to harvest clarum easily. They had been steadily walking toward that location since the sun had risen this morning. Scilla kept her nearly empty, expandable bag close at all times and intended to fill it up with as much clarum as she could stuff inside it when they reached the specified location.

After spending the time that she had in Patten, Scilla decided that even though she had grown up on Tendyis, her home was on Krael. Too many years had passed, and time had changed the people and the places, including herself. Her home was with the people that she had bonded with over time and who she valued in her heart. Home was with the people she loved and who loved her in return. It was good to come back and see her past for a while, but when she truly looked within her soul, she felt the most comfortable and happy surrounded by her friends on Krael. And so, to Krael she would return. Even if she could not retain her future sight for some reason, she would choose to be surrounded by the feelings of home on Krael.

Up ahead, Scilla heard the sound of rushing water. River Rial. The librarian had said that the clarum deposit was not far after crossing the river. The tangled trees had vibrant vines draping low enough to kiss the water's frothing surface. Beautiful flowers bloomed brilliantly in the trees, glowing orange, yellow, green, and blue. The light that they emitted bounced playfully in the river, and Scilla could see the shimmering sparkle beneath the swirls. She stopped before the water's edge to take in the unique sight. The others joined her, just as impressed.

Elasche knelt and scooped up a handful of the pretty water to look more closely. She eyed it with a curious smile, tilting it in various directions to watch the colorful light sparkle in slightly different ways through the water. Before Scilla could stop her, she put her cupped hands to her lips and drank a few sips.

"No!" Scilla shouted, "Don't drink the water!" but it was too late. Elasche looked up at her, and after a few seconds, her eyes went vacant as she passed out and flopped to the ground. Dainn was at her side immediately doing anything he could to try and wake Elasche up. Shaking, rubbing, shouting, and even delicately opening her eyes with his fingertips so he could see them staring at nothing.

"What happened to her? What is wrong with the water?" Dainn implored while clutching Elasche's body to his own as he knelt on the ground to hold her.

Scilla pointed upstream to a large cave where the river snaked out from. "That cave is rich with mineral deposits. The waters flowing through there have accumulated high volumes of mineral concentrate. High enough volumes that they are poisonous to a human. After the water has flowed downstream for a while, the mineral deposits are diluted, and the water is drinkable, but here…" Scilla trailed off and looked at Elasche. "I can't use my Spirit to heal her because I don't know the composition or concentration of the minerals in the water that poisoned her. There could be dangerous consequences if I try to purify her incorrectly. We need to cross the river. There is a friendly buflog tribe nearby who have natural remedies for this. Well, at least, many years ago, there used to be."

"Then we must go to them," Dainn said as he stood, carrying Elasche's unconscious body like a limp rag doll with her knees over his left arm and her head laying on his right shoulder. "How much time does she have?"

Scilla shook her head. She didn't know. She didn't know how concentrated the minerals were in the waters or how they had changed over time. Back in her days here, about twenty-four hours would have been the approximate timeframe, but she didn't want to scare Dainn anymore, so Scilla just said, "We must hurry," and then looked to Anik.

Anik was ready for the cue, and he used his knowledge of the natural elements to raise the flowing river into an arch tall enough that their tallest member, Dainn, could stand beneath it without ducking. The river waters continued to flow unperturbed, living creatures included, but in a path that allowed the group to cross underneath it. Droplets of water fell onto their heads as they traversed the muddy, rocky riverbed, but all of them were careful to wipe the water away lest any of it get into their mouths. "Watch for sandy sinkholes," Anik warned, causing Scilla to wonder how many times he had done this and what trouble he had encountered in the past. None of that mattered though, as he held the river high and sturdy above them. Once they were across, Anik gently placed the rushing river back onto its course.

"The buflogs used to fish here, and I think they still do," Scilla said as she pointed out some large amphibian-looking tracks in the muddied soil and a log that had been conveniently placed near the edge of the river, likely as a place to sit. Dainn nodded in response, his face masked in his usual stoic expression, although his actions all indicated his deep concern for Elasche's condition.

Scilla searched the depths of her memory for the location of the buflog's home. She had often waved to the friendly creatures as she had passed by here with her night mare as a child. They were frog-like creatures that were only about three-quarters the size of a fully grown human. They walked on two legs and generally wore homespun, neutral-colored tunics. Their large frog heads had the characteristic tongue that could slurp a bug out of the air or even a small fish from the river. Their eyes glowed yellow in the forest, and their fingers and toes glowed with red suction-cup endings extending out from their bodies of various shades of un-glowing green. She knew none of them would recognize her now, but she hoped their demeanor had remained the same over the years. They had always been kind and willing to help.

Scilla examined the tracks in the mud and then used her Spirit to trace where they had come from. She knew what a buflog track looked like and how big their steps were. Using that knowledge, her Spirit traced out a recent track and followed its subsequent tracks down a small forest path. It was damp, and the leaves of the bushes and ferns continuously slapped her face and arms as she made her way, slightly hunched, through the forest trail with her friends following. Scilla pulled a few narrow, long leaves from the plants surrounding her and began weaving them together in the shape of a star. It was something that she had done as a child and had offered as a gift to some buflogs that she had met. They had liked it, so she figured it wouldn't hurt to have a gift ready for the buflogs on arrival.

The path eventually opened into a clearing, and what she saw amazed her. The buflog town was recessed into a dig-out of clarum deposit. The path they were on swerved down the edge of the dig out a couple of times, but it wasn't too deep or too steep for them to follow. The town looked almost comfy in its little alcove. Unless coming from this very trail, it was camouflaged well into the surrounding forest, and there looked to only be this trail entering, unless someone wanted to vertically scale the walls of the clarum deposit.

All the huts here were made from stacked stone, clay, and mud. Their roofs were large leaf fronds woven together and placed overlapping each other on top of the stone structures. One side of each dwelling was built slightly taller than the other side, allowing for the roof to slope in one direction. The lines of houses were placed so that the roofs spilled the water into a stream between rows. That stream flowed toward the center of the buflog's town and into a large pond with bright green lily pads growing gorgeous, floppy, neon flowers out of their centers. The streams came from all sides of the town, like beams of a starburst coming together at their star in the center of the pond. At the end of the pond furthest from the entrance, overlooking the beautiful centerpiece, was the largest dwelling. Scilla knew this to be the chief's home, and she made her way there.

The town was bustling with buflogs who eyed the newcomers curiously. Some stopped their gardening, others paused their conversations, and others began whispered conversations. It was obvious that humans were not normal visitors to this town, but they were not altogether unwelcome. When they reached the door of the chief's house, they found it open. "Come in," Came a deep, croak-like voice that drew out the vowel sounds in words slowing down his speech drastically.

Scilla pushed the door open cautiously and saw a rather comfortable looking home. Dainn bowed his head to the chief buflog, who was a bit chunkier than the others that they had seen in town, before setting Elasche down on some pillows that had been stacked in a corner.

"I heard the town's whispers that you were here and that one of you is ill," the slow voice continued as an aging buflog stood up from his plush, comfortable-looking chair using a walking stick to prop himself up. "It is not often we have visitors; would you mind if I took a look at the girl?" He asked as he made his way over to Elasche.

"Please do," Scilla said, "She drank from the waters of River Rial outside the cave entrance. I fear she has been poisoned. I remembered…I mean, I heard, that your tribe may have a remedy for such an accident?" The buflog paused his stroll over to Elasche to look at Scilla. Scilla proffered her woven starburst leaves to the old creature who reached out his soft, amphibious hand and took it. He looked upon it and smiled.

"Call me Pog," he said in response before sitting down on the floor to look at Elasche. Scilla paused at that name. Something about it was familiar, but buflogs, long-lived as they were, didn't live as long as she had. She pushed that thought from her mind.

"I can help," he said after inspecting his patient. He pulled out some strong-smelling herbs along with a mortar and pestle from pockets that he had on his ornate, chiefly tunic. After making a paste, he took a swab of it onto his finger and placed it in her mouth between her teeth and cheek. "She needs time now; she will be okay. A bad taste in her mouth will be all that plagues her."

"Thank you, so much for this kindness," Scilla said. "What do we owe you?"

"Ah, silly strangely still young girl, asking for an unknown price for a task completed. Do you not remember? You have already paid for this task." Pog pulled out a necklace that was hidden beneath his tunic. The charm at the end was a starburst woven from decaying leaves. Some sort of enchantment must have been placed upon the weaving for it to have lasted this long, assuming it was the same one that Scilla had created many years ago. "You saved my father, also known as Pog. He taught me to remember you and to help others without asking a price. Without your quick actions pulling him out of the river and bringing him back to town for healing from ingesting the poisoned waters, he would have died, and I would not have existed. You asked for no payment then, and as such, I ask for no payment now."

Scilla remembered now. The Pog from long ago waved to her as he fished, and then he tripped over something into the river. Scilla had jumped off her night mare and reached into the water, hanging perilously over the edge, to pull him out onto her side of the river. He had already ingested too much water, so she and her night mare had crossed the river and followed his fishing buddies back to town. She had given Pog the starburst long before that day, in friendship. He must have kept it all these years and passed it on to his son. She never knew how much that trinket had meant to him.

"My deepest and sincerest thanks is how we pay you," Scilla responded. "It is nice to meet you, Pog. I am sure your father would be proud of you."

Pog smiled again, "It is of no matter. Please rest while your friend heals. What brings you out here, Scilla? It has been many years."

"I fear I come asking another favor of you, Pog. I come asking to harvest some of the clarum deposit that surrounds your town."

"A favor *from* me, you say? It sounds like a favor *to* me. An offer to expand my town's walls. We have been steadily growing. It would help to have a bit more space around here. Do you have a way of carving out the rock?" Pog inquired.

"Anik can use his magic to do that. Is there a place that you would prefer us to begin from?" Scilla replied eagerly, unable to believe her luck. Was one good deed so long ago worth this karma?

"Yes, young one, I will show you. Harvest as much as you need. I will have the buflog builders begin gathering for the building of new dwellings. What a great day this is turning out to be! We shall celebrate with a hearty evening meal. I do love meals." Pog said as he patted his wobbling belly, causing Scilla to chuckle slightly.

***

"Hmmm…" Zen wondered aloud, "I wonder." He scrounged through his hoard of magical artifacts in his makeshift living space and hoped that he had brought the one that he was looking for with him from Krael. He had taken to talking to himself lately since there weren't any real beings for him to have conversations with on Tendyis. Well, no beings of his intellectual level that wouldn't try to return him to exile if he revealed himself to them. In his mind, the self-talking helped to keep him sane, and it had the bonus of keeping his voice from getting scratchy from underuse. On Krael, his underlings and creatures that he manipulated in exchange for notes on their future provided ample conversation material, but here on Tendyis, where he was constantly on the run, there was no one for him to interact with. It was hard for Zen to admit it to himself, but he was lonely. Maybe he should get a pet.

"Oh, now that would be entertaining…a pet. I've never had one of those before. That could be a new experiment. It would have to be small and portable, and of course, extremely obedient," Zen mused as he continued to rummage. Images of small creatures bounded across his mind as he repeatedly reached into the satchel, scrutinized each object that he pulled out, and then tossed them behind him haphazardly onto a growing pile on the floor. Priceless historic objects and relics of immense and obscene magical power were cast aside like toys a child was bored of playing with. "A kitten, maybe? To stroke on my lap while I plot.

No. They are too independent. How about a bird? No. No. No. Too much chatter. A small reptile? A lizard or snake, perhaps? Possible. Dogs are trainable, but they are just far too happy. Squirrels? A ferret?"

Clink, clank, plop, went the items from the satchel until finally, "Aha! There you are! I knew I had brought you." Zen held up a small cylindrical object that looked like a short brass straw with some inscriptions on it. Compared to the pile of artifacts on the floor, it looked particularly unimpressive. From his studies, he knew that past owners of the artifact thought it could suck the souls out of the creatures it was used upon. Zen had other ideas though. If magical properties could live in stones and be used to infuse their corresponding beings with power, could the flow of magic go the other way? Could a creature's magic be sucked away from them and stored elsewhere? If that was done quickly enough, could that not feel to the victim as though their very soul was being sucked away since each creature's magic seemed to be intimately intertwined with who they were? Zen would find out. He would experiment and become even more powerful with his new knowledge! Now, if only he could find something to run some tests on.

Zen started cramming his artifacts back into his satchel before doing anything else. He couldn't take the chance that he may have to leave quickly and possibly leave his treasures behind. They were too valuable to him. Once that task was done, he let his thoughts wander again. Too bad he didn't have that pet now. Animals likely had some sort of magic that he could use. Or maybe they didn't, and that could have been a baseline for his experiments. Zen sighed; he would use himself. It was worth the possible sacrifice, if his theory was correct, and Zen had the utmost confidence in himself. He could always retrieve the magic back in reverse so long as it didn't really suck out any of his soul. He knew his magic's mineral was clarum from his trips down the futures of Scilla's mind. After a brief search, he had found samples of it in patches around the Plain of Portals and had cached the clarum in the shrubbery outside his hut.

Zen poked his head outside the door to the small hut near the Plain of Portals cautiously, looking all ways, making sure he couldn't see anyone. He could never be too careful these days. He made his way outside quickly and crouched behind a bush where he couldn't be seen well. He picked up a few pieces of the loose rocks on the surface near the bush's base and brought them inside. He noted how deep of a black each stone was in color before placing them on the table next to the brass straw with curious markings. He believed that the markings on the straw indicated the direction that the magic would flow into and out of it. He just had to decipher them.

After a while of pondering, Zen's patience ran out, and he decided just to try it. He would have to suck the magic out himself at some point, and it was easy enough to get it back from his clarum stash near the bush. He noted to himself that he would like to get more of the mineral before he tried to go back to Krael. He didn't want to risk running out again. But before he could return, those groundlings would need to get him the cloak of Ghaleon! Terrible conversation material those critters were, but they were all he had to work with for now.

Zen placed his finger lightly on a small indent near the marking on the straw. He aligned one end with himself and the other with the clarum. Immediately, he noticed a pinprick feeling on his chest at the location where the straw was pointing, and he started gasping as a strange sensation of emptiness collapsing in on itself began to overtake him. He pressed harder with his finger on the straw, and the pain became excruciating. He fell to the floor, breaking the line of sight of the straw to his chest. The pain subsided, but an echo of pain remained, and his head felt a little foggy. He put his empty hand on his chest as he regained his breath before standing to put the straw back onto the table.

The sight before him on the table left him astonished. The clarum pieces had undoubtedly darkened. They had filled with his magic! Zen felt excitement bubble up at his discovery. He hadn't felt like this since a child, experimenting alone in his bedroom. Other memories seemed to knock on a door in Zen's mind at that thought, but he rejected them behind tall and thick walls that had been constructed and strengthened over time, instead, he focused on just the experiments that he had done and the pleasure that they had brought him. Back in his current time, Zen eagerly reached out to the clarum on the table, and when he touched it, he felt a pleasant, warm, fulfilling feeling as his powers returned to him, lightening the stone. Zen had been right. He could control the flow of magic!

Knock, knock, knock, came a noise from the lower half of the door to Zen's little hut, disrupting Zen's groundbreaking moment. At first, he was irritated, but then a thought struck him, "The groundlings!" Zen thought excitedly. He was not sure how this day could get much better. The creature must be here to give him the cloak of Ghaleon! Just to be safe, Zen carefully peeked out of the curtained window before answering the door. Yes, it was indeed the groundling that he had asked to deliver Ghaleon's cloak to him, but he didn't seem to have anything in tow. That worried Zen a little, but he opened the door to the small creature to see what it had to say.

The groundling backed away at Zen's imposing presence, and its body quivered slightly as it kept its head lowered, refusing to meet Zen's eyes. Zen noticed that the groundling did not glow out here as it had in the forest where he had first met them. Its coloring was mute and mundane in the normal light. If it had stood still in the darkness, one would have had a hard time spotting it.

"My cloak?" Zen implored while gazing upon the small creature with disdain.

“It’s…uh…we had cloak…uh…then cloak taken,” the groundling stuttered, stringing together words that Zen did not like.

“Speak clearly. Where is my cloak?” Zen’s voice was not risen, but he spoke powerfully with an air of authority that the groundling would feel compelled to obey.

“Cloak stolen. Sorry Mister,” the groundling cowered and shrieked as an angered Zen slammed the door shut at this response.

“Be gone!” Zen ordered, and he heard the creature immediately scurry away. As with anything that he needed done correctly, Zen would have to do this himself. Zen plopped down on a wooden rocking chair to begin planning. He had to find where that cloak was and go get it himself. His wonderful day had just been utterly ruined. Zen wondered to himself why he could never catch a break. Zen shook his head. He assuredly did not want a groundling for a pet.

Chapter 14

"Nico!" Vi let out a long, exaggerated cry of his name. "You are sending us in circles! I see the bite I took out of that fruit on that tree ages ago!" Vi pointed toward a bunch of purple berries that did have a distinctive bite mark missing from them as juices oozed onto the forest floor.

Nico shrunk down his overly large ears at Vi's criticism, but they bounced back up again quickly. "Nico smell him! Miran been here! Nico knows! Follow, follow!"

Vi rolled her eyes and hid back inside the pouch as the night mare plodded along with a bobbing head next to a skipping and humming Nico. He excitedly pointed out all the flowers and animals that they saw along the way telling the group what they were and what they were known for. He seemed intelligent on matters of the forest, and Mory was storing the information away for possible use later.

Mory was doing his best to humor Nico and Vi's interactions. They both sported extremely animated personalities, constantly feeding off each other's emotions. It was comical to a certain extent, but Mory couldn't help but agree with Vi's sentiment on this matter. Nico had been leading them around the forest for a couple of days now without success. They did find a magnificent white feather that looked like it could belong to the hunter's bird, but that was the only lead that they had so far.

Mory pulled up the night mare, and Nico skipped a few more steps before realizing that the group had halted. Mory had to re-vector this expedition, "Nico, let's say that Miran walks a lot of different paths in Bellis, especially if he lives here. Instead of just following where you can smell him. Can you follow the path where you smell him the strongest? Or maybe you can follow the scent of the bird and Miran combined?"

Nico cocked his head, contemplating Mory's words, then started jumping up and down gesturing toward himself, "Yes. Nico like idea. Give Nico feather." Nico took a deep breath, inhaling the scent of the bird, and then stood still, letting the quiet of the forest settle in around them as he oriented himself. He sniffed around the ground surrounding them in deep concentration before handing Mory back the feather with a proud look on his face. "This way!" Nico pointed to a path perpendicular to the circle that they had been traversing.

They may have been circling the correct location as opposed to closing in on it this whole time. That seemed plausible in Mory's mind. Nico was still rather young and inexperienced at many things. Tracking was likely new to him.

"Lead on Nico. We will follow you," Mory said encouragingly, but in his head, Mory was getting exhausted from the detour and hoped this was the last little push that they needed to find the hidden hunter and that they were not just chasing new phantoms. Nico scurried on ahead of them causing a kaleidoscope of neon-accented butterflies to flutter away from the fruit tree grove that he ran into. His big ears bobbed with his steps while happily leading the way.

***

Miran stroked Lucy's white feathers down her neck as he stood, facing her, outside his forest home. Her big head leaned slightly against his as they enjoyed each other's company. Her feathers smelled sweet and woody, like they had been kept in a cedar chest with a pile of dried rose petals. Miran found her scent just as relaxing as Lucy found his neck strokes. Her eyes were barely open, and she cooed softly as Miran scratched a nice spot beneath her chin.

Waiting was the worst. Miran had the cloak in his possession for a few days now, and yet no one had come to retrieve it. It didn't seem all that special to him. It was a nice durable cloak -white with a strange purple glow to it- but it didn't seem odd or magical to him in any obvious way. Glowing paraphernalia was common in Bellis. He had spent a good many hours examining it as well as he could without harming it. Miran did not know the exact purpose of the cloak because even though he could see the possible threads of the future, he could not see what people were thinking and why they were doing the things that he saw. If he had been able to read minds as well as see the future, he figured that he could better track his prey, following their logic for the choices they made.

Lucy had just brought in another couple of letters requesting his help this morning. His basket was starting to mound over. The increasing pile nagged at his conscious even more today than usual because he thought that he should be taking care of some of those requests as opposed to idling here. If he left, though, he might miss his opportunity to confront Kaitzen. He couldn't do that, so he let the request pile continue to grow, and he was petting Lucy to help calm his nerves. Lucy seemed to sense his anxiety, and she nuzzled his head affectionately. Miran couldn't help but smile. He was closer to Lucy than any other living creature, and they could sense each other's feelings well. Their bond was something unique and irreplaceable. Miran cherished her very much.

Miran caught movement in one of the large, blue-green bushes surrounding his living quarters out of the corner of his eye. He adjusted himself into a defensive position, and Lucy instinctively opened her wings to hide Miran beneath the wing that he was closest to as she stared down the intruder from the bushes with her big, hazel eyes. Miran peeked beneath Lucy's great wing to see who he immediately recognized as Scilla from his visions. He was surprised. His quarry had never just come to him, unprovoked. He had stopped tracing her future paths recently in order to focus on Kaitzen, so he had not foreseen her arrival.

The bush she had emerged from had some prickers in it, and they tugged at her loose black dress revealing sturdy, black hiking boots. Unbeknownst to Scilla, a bright, yellow flower had haphazardly pinned itself to her short black hair as she had made her way through the bushes. Miran was caught off guard by his feelings. Scilla hadn't been this pretty in his future site, had she? She was small in frame and careful of step but portrayed a confidence borne of experience. He had never seen someone so beautiful in his life.

"Excuse me, Miran, is it? I hope I didn't startle you," Scilla spoke as she pulled the prickers out of her clothing.

Miran nodded his head, cautiously emerging from behind Lucy's wing, and still not quite sure what to say to this woman who had enchanted him. Lucy eyed Scilla with a healthy level of mistrust, and Miran had to stroke her a few times to stop her feathers from sticking out like a startled hedgehog's quills, which they tended to do when she was riled up.

"Pog, from the buflog tribe across the Rial river, sent us to you with high commendations," Scilla explained. "He said that you help those in need and never fail regardless of the complexity and/or danger of the situation. I happen to have a situation that boasts of both attributes if you are available."

Miran remembered Pog, the kindly, old buflog chief. He had indeed helped their tribe on multiple occasions. Never with any particularly dangerous situations, but Pog was the sort of creature who would boast about someone else's capabilities. He would not have sent someone who meant Miran ill-will to his home. His mind chewed on Scilla's words before it focused on one. He pointed it out to Scilla, "Us? There are more of you?"

Scilla motioned with her hand, and two men and one girl made their way out of the bushes near her. Miran would have to watch the burlier man closely. He gave off the most dangerous vibes of the group, but the younger one had a fire in his eyes that wasn't common to Tendyians. He would be challenging in his own way. Scilla apologized, "I'm sorry, Miran, I didn't want to scare you with a multitude of people. We come in peace and mean you no harm."

Beautiful or not, Miran was not happy that she had hidden the others that she had brought from him. He crossed his arms and replied to her a bit defensively, "Anything else you are hiding? This is my home. I am not battle-ready, as you can see." Miran upturned the palms of his hands and turned around to show Scilla that he had no obvious weapons. He did have a small knife hidden in his leather leggings, but better safe than sorry.

"I meant no offense," Scilla pleaded with dignity. "I figured we were better safe than sorry. That bird of yours is a bit frightening, although stunning."

Miran halted his thoughts. Had she read his mind? She had spoken the same words that he had thought. Maybe she just reasoned like him? She was approaching unknown territory. He would have done the same in her circumstances.

Miran removed the defensive bite from his words and relaxed his arms into a more open posture, "The bird is a dewl named Lucy who is my friend. Forgive me for not being a better host. Please, sit down, and we can talk." Miran gestured to some overturned logs by a burnt-out fire pit that he frequently used to sit on while roasting food.

"Nice to meet you, Lucy. We thank you for your hospitality, Miran." Scilla bowed slightly before taking a seat, sharing a log with the younger man with orange-ish hair. The older, more intimidating-looking man sat with the other girl. "I am Scilla. This is Anik, Dainn, and Elasche," she said as she pointed each one out. "We come looking for our friends who ventured into this forest seeking a stolen cloak. Our friends are a boy and a girl roughly the same age, both with golden hair, likely traveling with a night mare. As for the cloak, it is a good quality piece, pure white of color with a purple essence about it. Have you run across the cloak or our friends, or could you help us find them?"

Miran hesitated. He wasn't sure whether to tell Scilla the truth or not about having the cloak here, or about having seen her companions near the groundling tribe. He cursed himself for not following the paths of the future with her in them. He couldn't let her take the cloak. Not without having captured Kaitzen first. He was also torn about having her in his custody. She was an exile too. She should be captured and… and… well what. Miran didn't know. She didn't seem to be a threat to Tendyis. He decided to buy himself time to think by elongating the conversation.

"What is so special about this cloak that you seek? Could you not just have another one made?" Miran inquired.

Scilla took the bait and responded, "It has magical powers that protect the wearer from death when traveling across space through the portals. We would like to go home to our planet and not meet our deaths along the way."

Miran was astonished. Not just by the type of magic that the cloak had, but because the exiles were trying to exile themselves again! On purpose! He also wasn't sure if he wanted Scilla to leave. That other planet was not her 'home.' She was from Tendyis, and any Tendyian would know that from her skin tone and consistency. Truthfully, a part of Miran wanted to get to know her better too. He didn't have much time, so he acted on instinct.

"I have a cloak that meets that description here. Come with me. I'll show you," he stated. Instead of leading them toward the main house where he had stashed the cloak into a trunk, he took them into a side hut where he stored food over the colder months of the year. He walked in and made a show of looking around to make sure no one else was watching. Once they were all inside, he slammed the door shut and locked them in by bracing a long board across the entryway. Miran needed to think. He wasn't going to hurt them. He just needed time to sort all this through.

***

The smell of salty meats and preserved fruit pastes would not have been all that unappealing if it hadn't been a part of their newly assigned prison. Scilla swung a few hanging meat carcasses out of the way while searching the outer walls of their confinement for a way out. She had her arms stretched upwards, palms on the wooden walls, and wore a small frown on her face as she tried to peek out a tiny window from her tiptoes. She could have probably fit both her arms through, but that was it. The window wasn't tall enough for her head to squeeze through too. Dainn was ramming the door with his shoulder, but the wood was very sturdy, even for his massive form. Anik was trying to pull him back, unsuccessfully, before he hurt himself. Scilla had not conceived that the man Pog had sent them to would imprison them. Maybe she had been too honest with Miran about the cloak.

Scilla waved Elasche over and asked for her help to prop her up a little bit so she could get a better look outside of the window. Once she had a steady viewpoint atop of Elasche's folded hands, to Scilla's surprise, she saw Mory jump out of the bushes with Kylie by his side. Their sword and daggers were drawn as they faced down Miran. Lucy protectively put herself between the ambushers and Miran as he raced toward his practice targets to grab his bow and quiver. Vi flew out of the woods, glowing purple, and succeeded in distracting Lucy long enough for Kylie to roll by her and meet a now ready Miran with an arrow nocked in his bow aimed straight for her.

Scilla heard Dainn grunt to get their attention. He had applied heat to the metal lock with his Koth, burning the wood around it just enough that he could weaken the door there. Then he had punched his way through in a poof of ashes and flung away the locking board that Miran had placed across the door. They were free! Elasche let Scilla hop down from her window perch and ran to Dainn to heal his bleeding knuckles with her Spirit.

"I'm going into the main house to look for the cloak," Scilla said. You guys help Kylie and Mory. Keep Miran and Lucy distracted for as long as you can. I have a hunch that he really does have the cloak, and I would like to look for it myself." The others nodded, and she made a run for the door of the house, picking her ankle-length dress up to her knees as she ran, trusting the others to take care of the fighting for her.

The door was unlocked, and the house was not very large. After glancing around, she saw a trunk that was slamming shut as the curtain of a nearby window was disturbed and fluttering unnaturally. She ran to the trunk and looked out the window to see none other than Kaitzen sprinting into the forest with Ghaleon's cloak and his ponytail streaming behind him. She gaped at him, not reacting fast enough to do anything. She paused for a moment, kneeling to re-open the trunk that must have previously held the cloak. It was empty. As she turned her head back up, the yellow flower fell from her hair and fluttered softly into the vacant trunk.

***

Zen ran. Oh, the feeling of the soft cloak's fabric in his hands gave him incredible amounts of glee. Even when he tripped over the windowsill and ate a decent-sized mouth full of dirt upon his exit, it had almost tasted like a decadent chocolate dessert in his mouth instead of earthy chunks. He flung the cloak over his shoulders and tied it around his chest as he ran back into the cover of the forest to find his bag of belongings.

This had not been his plan, but because of that, he had seen it as his best opportunity to succeed. This would not have been a highly probable path for his future to take if his future was being watched by another. When the skirmish had broken out between the groups at the hunter's home, Zen could not believe his luck. He had time to sneak in through the back window of the largest hut, and the trunk nearest to that window was unlocked and held the very treasure that he had so long desired. His hard work and perseverance had finally paid off!

When he got to his bag of belongings, which held all the possessions that he had taken to Tendyis, he pulled out his trusty teleporting rod and thought of his destination: the portal to Krael. His body winked out of existence while he traveled with his bag, and the next thing that he saw was the great swirl of ominous colors within the shining golden portal ring looming tall in front of him. He was paralyzed in fear. Memories from long ago pried angrily at his consciousness begging to be let out, clawing and tearing at the sanity within his mind as he fought to keep them caged.

As Zen wrestled with himself, Sonu appeared, solidifying himself into the corporeal world. Sonu snatched the cloak from Zen's back and grabbed him by the chest of his shirt to stare him in the eyes while slightly lifting him off the ground. Zen's eyes widened in shock, and he could feel himself still weak and quivering from his other fears. His mind could not process the new situation fast enough to respond with an adequate defense.

"You," Zen stammered as he tried in vain to at least get his tiptoes back onto the ground, "You're dead."

"Not completely," Sonu replied, and then before Zen could gain any sort of advantage back, Sonu pushed his old master tumbling into the interspace portal without the protection of Ghaleon's cloak.

***

Scilla had been trying to get the attention of anyone in the half-hearted battle at the hunter's hut. She jumped up and down, waved her arms, and shouted, hesitant to do anything drastic with her Spirit magic in case it turned the tides of the battle toward violence. Lucy and Miran were holding up well against four rivals. They were clearly not greenhorns to a fight. They were holding back on the lethal force of Lucy's beak and talons, as well as Miran's bow. No one seemed to want to hurt anyone, but no one really trusted their opponent not to hurt them either, so they were fully engrossed in sparring each other until Ghaleon's cloak appeared, hovering above them all, a flowing fabric in the breeze below the treetops. That was enough to get everyone's attention and stop the fighting as they made way for its glorious descent.

"What in the..." Mory started to say before the cloak landed in the center of Miran's yard, and Sonu appeared fully before them all with the cloak on his back.

Miran stood gaping, obviously never having seen a ghost become tangible before. Mory was incredibly excited and reached his hand toward Sonu to have his cloak returned to him. Scilla was devastated and visibly deflated at the sight.

"Kaitzen?" she asked Sonu. "What happened to him?" Deep down she had an inkling, but she wanted him to say the words, just in case.

"He went through the portal, once again," Sonu declared.

"But you have the cloak," Scilla pointed out.

Sonu explained softly, noting Scilla's somber state, "Yes, I took it from him before he escaped, so you guys could get back to Krael safely."

"But that means..." Scilla started to say before Sonu cut her off.

"It means that Kaitzen's life was left up to fate once more. He is strong in magic, even if incorrigible in his evil ways.

If you wish to see him again on Krael, I will bet that he is there waiting for you. Although, he is likely not waiting idly. He will be re-engaging with his old contacts and stirring up trouble in every way possible. You should get back soon to protect Krael. Not everyone will be as lenient with him as your heart is, Scilla. He has wronged many a soul on Krael. You know this."

"I do. I very much do," Scilla acknowledged Sonu's logic before picking herself up and turning to her friends. "Let's gather ourselves and make ready for leaving tomorrow. Miran deserves to know our story for the trouble that we've caused him and his house if he will have us over for the evening."

Miran looked at them with a silent pause before accepting the offer, "Yes, I would enjoy hearing your stories for the evening. It is not often that I have company beyond Lucy. I am a hunter of exiles and knowing that Kaitzen is gone from Tendyis and that you plan on returning to the planet that you were exiled to in the first place means that my duty is complete. I can spend the evening in respite without guilt. I have food enough for us all to make up for the breach in hospitality that I showed you before if you accept my offer."

They all nodded hungrily from their eventful days, and Miran started putting them to work on the necessary chores to get ready for their dinner.

Dainn approached Scilla as they were gathering sticks of kindling for the fire in order to break some news to her, "Elasche and I will need to return to Mahashta when we are back on Krael. There is something that I must attend to there, based upon what I have learned on our travels here."

Scilla nodded understandingly as she tucked another small, dry stick into her armful. Dry sticks were proving hard to find, so she was using bits of her Spirit to draw the moisture out when she collected them. "I would never dream of keeping you against your will, Dainn, and the help that you have already given us has been plenty. Please return to your people and do what you must. Let me know if there is anything that I can do to assist you."

Dainn's stick bundle was of much larger pieces than Scilla's, but they knew both sets of wood would be useful, "Scilla, you are the one who has enlightened me on our travels and has given me hope in something that I thought lost for so long. I will return to you and help you reunite with Kaitzen once I follow my leads back home. I reckon you will need time to gather yourselves when back on Krael. I will just be filling in the time between now and then."

"As you wish," Scilla accepted Dainn's offer to return. "It would be remiss of me to not accept any offerings of help you grant for my dealings with Kaitzen. Good luck with your endeavors in Mahashta."

"Thank you, Scilla. Good luck to you as well. I know well the value of a sibling you care for. Your feelings are not alone," Dainn reassured Scilla while shuffling his stick armful to allow him to put his large hand on her tiny shoulder in a rare show of affection from the man.

The forest came alive with brighter colors and animal chatter as the night went on. The smell of the seasoned meat and fruit cooked over the fire was only rivaled in mouthwatering deliciousness by the taste of the finished product. The group of friends regaled each other with stories bringing them closer together before turning in for a well-deserved night's sleep. They agreed that they should meet again sometime since Ghaleon's cloak allowed them to do so without peril.

Chapter 15

Days later, back on Krael, in the realm of Mahashta, the first sun was just disappearing over the horizon relinquishing her warmth from the desert evening. Dainn walked swiftly past the sparring fields onto the back of the archery range holding himself as collected as he could with the feelings of urgency bursting out of him. He spotted Lancet alone on the range, as he had hoped, around the evening mealtime. Lancet's black ponytail flicked ever so slightly as he released his drawn arrow which moments later made a satisfying *thwack* in the center of the furthest target. As the arrow found its mark, Dainn approached his target as well, hoping that the other arrow's bullseye was an omen for his success…or at least for the mood of his old friend to be boosted momentarily for the upcoming conversation. He was Dainn's best hope to bring back Denna and the others if only he would cooperate.

Dainn stopped a respectful distance away, bowed slightly at his hips with his head down, and announced himself before getting too close, "Good evening, Lancet. Could you spare a moment for a few words?"

Lancet cringed slightly before turning his head away from the target range to look toward Dainn. He glanced at him over his shoulder and out of the corner of his slightly narrowed eyes. "There's not much to say, Dainn, nor much I'd like to hear from you," Lancet's voice was sharp and distrusting before he sighed, turned completely about, and finished his thought, "but if you are speaking, you must deem it important. Out with it."

The words and actions stung Dainn deeply, but he knew he deserved them for losing Denna and his other friends so many years ago. He would resolve that soon. He would redeem himself. He needed Lancet at his side to do just that. Dainn summoned his Koth ever so slightly to calm the sting in his heart and straightened his back to look Lancet in the eyes before beginning his plight. "I think I know how we can save Denna and the others."

Now he had Lancet's attention. He saw the spark of hope flit across his eyes before the shadow of disbelief darkened them once more. Lancet didn't respond, so Dainn carried on, "The portals, I think each instance may be linked to historic events. Time warps of a sort. They take the Ignet who enter them back to some trial that occurred in the past, and we have to resolve it once more to pass and return to our time. I think I ran across the historical place of the trial we failed. I now know how that dilemma was historically resolved. All we must do is re-enact those events, and we should be able to pass. Those Spirit wielders that we fought so hard to take down at the time were our *allies*. We needed to free them from the mind-boggling spell upon them, and then take down the beast. With an increased number of formidable allies at our side we could have taken it down!"

A flare of anger boiled out of Lancet, "Now you want to go back and earn the power that would have been granted to us from passing the trial that killed our friends? I knew you were ashamed of the loss, but I never thought you were an ambitious man, greedy for power..."

"Stop!" Dainn shouted uncharacteristically before Lancet could come up with any other wild accusations. Lancet was stunned to silence for just long enough for Dainn to regain his turf. Dainn softened his voice to normal tones once more, "It's a time warp, Lancet. My proposition is that you and I go in together. We take two out of the five slots, and then we find and bring back our friends with the other three open slots after completing the trial. My theory is that time will back up to the instant when the trial starts. A time when our friends were alive. It *has* to. How else could other Ignet re-do the same trials? I do not understand this time magic, but it must be how it works. I have convinced myself of it."

Lancet was considering Dainn's words, "How did you come to know this? Why should I believe you?"

"I was on the planet Tendyis, and we came across the ruins of an old battlefield. I was fortunate enough to have a knowledgeable scholar with me at the time to enlighten me on the history. I returned as soon as I could to save them."

Lancet was visibly disturbed by all this. "First you expect me to believe in time warps, which you nearly had me with, Dainn, but now you expect me to believe that you've been gallivanting about to other planets in search of this answer? No, this is too much. I cannot believe you. I cannot trust you. You have proven yourself untrustworthy in the past. There is no reason for me to believe you now."

"Please Lancet, would you reconsider? I think you and I have the best chance of saving them. We may need the exact same people who entered to exit. I don't know the exact details of how it all works. I am just grasping at possibilities at this point to atone for my past and retrieve those we've thought lost."

Dainn was not above begging at this point, but it didn't seem to matter. Lancet turned and stormed away, waving a dismissive hand over his head. "No, Dainn. I will not believe the stories you weave to try and save your soul. Count me out."

Dainn watched as Lancet strode away back toward the mess hall. The light of hope had dimmed within, and the world felt immensely heavy. He knew he would try anyway. He had to. He could not live with himself if he didn't at least try, but he knew his chances of success were now significantly decreased. As he stood there wallowing in the despair of defeat, he saw a small feminine figure approach him. He wondered how long she had been watching.

"I'll come with you." A determined Elasche said. "I heard your plea to Lancet. I am ready to take his place. I know Lancet was your first choice, but if he refuses to go, then what can it harm if I go along? I know the history. I understand what has to be done. I have the ability to disperse the spell on the Spirit wielders. I can do it. We can do it…together."

"No, I cannot risk the one I swore to protect. It would be folly to lose you too." Dainn responded instinctively.

"And now you sound like Lancet." Elasche rolled her eyes and shook her head.

Dainn paused and thought about it for a moment as he watched the last sun set beyond the desert horizon. She was right. "Thank you, Elasche. Your help would be greatly appreciated."

They watched the bright pink color fade into a dark purple before giving way to the deep blue of the night before making their way to the Elder's Circle to request permission to undertake their trial.

***

Dainn was nervous as he addressed the Elders, but he stated his case anyway. He was honest about his circumstances, which was always a befitting way to treat them. They had ways of knowing when someone was not being completely honest. Elasche knelt beside him with her head bowed respectively for the duration of Dainn's request. The Elder's silent caucus was much longer than Elasche's first trial. Dainn could see Elasche nodding off ever so slightly as the night went on. Dainn watched the Elders as their bodies remained motionless in their cross-legged positions on their mats. They didn't even bat an eyelid. It was obvious that their minds were convening elsewhere.

Finally, their heads slowly bobbed up in unison, and together they spoke their mind, "You will undertake the trial you have requested. Upon your success or defeat, it is requested that you, Dainn, return to us. We are interested in your knowledge of the portals and what else you may learn on your trial. This is the second time in short succession that you bring us interesting information on the portals. The first being of their construction of flarium and the stone's connection to our Koth. Go with our blessing and bring back those you have lost…including yourself. We are very interested in your findings. Another visitor will be arriving here soon. Rest well before your trial commences." And with that, the Elders disappeared into their mysterious smoke swirls.

***

The walk to the tunnels the next day was unusually awkward. People gathered to watch, but there was not the usual exciting buzz. There were hesitant whispers and sidelong worried glances sprinkled with some shaking heads. Dainn realized that they all must know, somehow, that the lone two of them, one a princess, would be entering a high-level trial meant for 5 people. Lancet must have told them. Dainn sighed heavily and looked to Elasche to see how she was handling the situation. She had her head cocked high as she used her staff as a walking pole, her eyes staring at the entrance to the tunnels ahead. It was as if the crowds surrounding them did not exist to her. He took to heart her example and did his best to keep his focus ahead while subconsciously filling his role of protector, panning the crowd for anyone who may have been attempting to harm Elasche.

At the end of their walk, the two gate guards bowed to them, parting to allow access to the tunnel entrance. The Rose Gates let both of the trial combatants in with ease before they disappeared into the tunnel's darkness as white-robed specs. The familiar sweet, spicy smell of the ceremonial incense was comforting to Dainn as he traversed the tunnels. Once more, he was accosted by the pain of old memories from the last time that he had attempted this trial. Through the pain, he felt the light brush of a soft hand before it squeezed his own. He looked down to his side to see Elasche smiling up at him to ease his woes. At first, the de ja vu was too much, but he used the flow of Koth to settle his emotions before returning the smile and squeeze before letting go of her hand.

The tunnels opened up into the portal area, and Dainn headed straight for his destination without hesitation. Once he approached the portal, he was taken aback by what he saw. Lancet was sitting cross-legged on the dirt floor in a meditative stance awaiting their arrival.

"Finally, you made it. I thought we always did these things early in the morning?" Lancet greeted them with a slight nod of his head before standing up and brushing off the dirt from his white garb.

Dainn, hesitated before replying, still stunned by what he was seeing. "I…uh…thought it best Elasche and I come into the trial well rested. The asking of the elders took longer than anticipated last night. How…Why…I mean, Lancet you're here?"

"Ha ha ha! Yes, I decided that it was worth the chance. I approached the elders after you and made my own request. They accepted immediately after thinking so long about your request. Per their instruction, I am to ask Elasche if it is all right if I take her place even though the elders previously gave her permission to enter the portal trial." Lancet bowed deeply to Elasche with this request.

Dainn looked to Elasche with a look of plea in his eyes before she could respond, "You are strong, Elasche, and I would be honored to take you in by my side, but I think the best chance to save my old friends is to bring the same colleague along that we failed with the first time."

Elasche waved her hand about to hush Dainn before he could go any further, "Yes, of course! I will await your return. Please, be careful. Remember that coming back with fewer people than you entered the portal with is not an ideal course. You need to be alive and well to help your friends out any further."

With that, Elasche took a seat on a large rock nearby, and Lancet straightened himself. Lancet and Dainn grasped hands in camaraderie and grunted in a determined fashion before turning to the swirling colors of the portal. They placed their hands on two of the five open circles along the edge of the cold portal gate creating their two white orbs within the swirling, rainbow vortex inside the gate. Dainn thought he may have seen the ghostly shapes of three other white orbs dancing in the distance before merging with the two solid ones just created by Dainn and Lancet. It could have been a trick of the rainbow portal light, or it could have been real. That thought gave him the strength he needed to raise his hand to indicate the hardest level of trial, replicating the exact same circumstances from which he had last entered. With a resolved look in their eyes, Dainn and Lancet stepped in unison into the portal and vanished.

Dainn rolled out of the portal transport onto the same grassy field filled with the same menagerie of creatures that they had encountered before. He sat for a moment to let the portal sickness fade before accepting Lancet's outstretched hand to help him stand up. The same horrific storm brewed in the distance, and Dainn knew the real trouble lay within that gray mess of chaos.

"Let's look around the camp. Maybe they are here with the rest of these creatures." Dainn suggested. Lancet and Dainn began looking for familiar faces amongst the crowd at the war camp but saw none. They did catch snippets of conversations indicating that a group of Spirit wielders had gone to take down the source of the unnatural storm.

"I am starting to believe your story now, Dainn." Lancet spoke, "These people are talking of the Spirit wielders as their fellow soldiers. Some speak of them with reverence due to heroes. If only…" Lancet's sentence caught in his throat before the rest came out. He didn't need to finish it. Dainn understood and felt his own conscience bite. If only they had remained in camp and listened to the group here before going on the hunt the first time that they had entered the trial, maybe they would have figured out the real solution and everyone would have come back alive.

"It's too late now for regrets, Lancet," Dainn responded. "We do what we must to set right the mistakes of our past. You have the mark that enables the de-fuddling of another's mind?"

"Yes. I've used it a few times before with success."

"Even on magically induced befuddlements?" Dainn inquired deeper.

"Yes."

"Good, then we are prepared. There should be three good Spirit-wielding humans in that storm if I remember correctly, and I do not forget a moment of that day. Let's try to communicate when we've turned each one. I'm hoping that we find our friends before we meet any of the Spirit wielders, but best for us to go in prepared this time." Dainn finished his thoughts before looking off to the storm once more.

Lancet replied, "I agree. I don't think we can get any more information here. Let's approach that storm. If we haven't found Denna, Rosco, or Grymm by the time we breach the rains, let's try to make for the locations…the locations where they last fell."

Dainn nodded his agreement, and they both made their way across the grassy field to the magical storm. The winds blew so strongly as they approached that the grass beneath their feet seemed permanently bent in a diagonal direction. Both Lancet and Dainn's tattoos began to glow, and the ferocity of the storm bent around them so they could better navigate their surroundings. They looked to each other, one last time, before crossing the magical line of the storm where the rain began to pour out of the clouds like a sporadic waterfall. Dainn thought he could feel the resolution in Lancet's stare. It was the same in his own heart. They would not fail this time. They would come back with their lost comrades.

Dainn launched himself into the sheet of rain. His enchantment kept the rain from his eyes, and he even impressed himself with how well he remembered the lay of the land here from that day. He found the slight hill in the terrain where he had last seen Denna. His heart pounded with anticipation as he neared the top which warmed his body in the chilly raindrops. His feet felt heavier and heavier as he plodded uphill. He wasn't sure what he would do if she wasn't there. There was no next path he could take that was planned. Before the suspense could weigh anymore on him, Dainn, with one quick burst of speed, crested the hill and looked around. She was there. Denna was there.

"Denna!" Dainn shouted through the heavy rain and wind, "Denna, thank all that is good. I've found you!" Dainn fell to his knees in front of the girl who was sitting cross-legged in front of him with her wet hair plastered to her face and neck.

"Dainn! I… I feel very confused. Like I am living in a scene from the past. I remember us coming here to earn another tattoo, but I feel the weight of failure heavily upon my soul. I didn't see any of you, and I don't remember how I got here from the portal. I sat here for a bit to try to piece together my mind before moving on."

Dainn hugged the girl harder than he had anticipated which earned him an "Umph" after he cut off her words. "I'll explain later, Denna. For now, let's find our friends and complete this trial. We need to un-fuddle the minds of the Spirit wielder humans and get them on our team to fight the source of this storm. How is your Koth energy level? Are you feeling strained at all?"

"My Koth is well. I have not used much at all other than to block the rain and cold." Denna responded.

"Excellent." Dainn nodded.

That was all Denna needed to regain composure. Dainn helped the girl up, and they surveyed the area as well as they could in the storm. Dainn spotted a man standing near the base of the hill on the opposite side of where he had ascended. It was Rosco. That was where he had fallen when he had fought off the monster to allow Lancet to drag Dainn's half-dead, sorry self away from the danger. Dainn jogged carefully down the slick grass of the hill to Rosco's side.

Rosco was holding his head in both hands and shaking it slowly from side to side when Dainn reached him.

"Dainn? I don't understand why I am surprised to see you, but I am." Rosco greeted him.

"I know you feel confused right now, but please trust me for a moment, Rosco. We need to alter our plans. I have new information to counter our original ones. We need to act quickly. I will explain everything once we achieve our objectives. Essentially, we need to convert the Spirit-wielding humans to our side before we take on the source of this storm, or we will fail. They have a mind-boggling magic spell on them. They are on our side if we can lift the spell."

"You seem…different, Dainn." Rosco squinted his eyes, examining Dainn's face closely. "Of course. That plan seems just as well as killing them. It would definitely make taking whatever the creature is creating this storm easier to have more allies."

Lightning cracked down from the sky and three figures were illuminated running toward them. Two wore cloaks and the other had a bow slung across his back. Lancet must have found two of the Spirit wielders and converted them already.

Lancet reached the group panting with a few streaks of blood across his face. Denna instantly remedied the situation before he could speak. Lancet's eyes drifted toward Denna at the touch of her Koth, and his eyes lit up with an untold number of emotions, a strange combination of vigor and softness that Dainn had not seen in years. Lancet froze for a moment looking into her eyes before collecting himself and introducing the people with him. "We've earned two more allies. The third is probably closer to Ramanatra. That is the name of the enemy we are fighting in the storm."

Dainn recognized the Spirit wielders as the two that he had fought in the previous battle. He remembered the man's face and the tendrils of blonde hair escaping the confines of the woman's hood.

"We thank you for saving us from Rama's spell. Please help us find our friend, and we will help you take Rama down," spoke the blonde woman in a heavy accent that was unfamiliar to Dainn as she bowed her head slightly in thanks.

Rosco immediately took charge, "Of course! We have one more friend out there too. Let's go further into the storm to investigate. We will save proper introductions for when we are safe." He drew his swords from their sheaths and started walking deeper into the darkness followed by the rest of the slowly growing group.

A loud roar, shriller than the booming thunder, came from up ahead. A timely streak of lightning revealed Grymm already in combat with the wolf-cat being, Ramanatra. Poor Grymm. It made sense that he would have fallen, and as-such been revived at the feet of the beast. Dainn only hoped that his confusion did not last for long before the beast attacked him. Dainn and Rosco ran in while Lancet set up his bow. Dainn enhanced his strength and agility with this Koth as he approached the monster. Before he could close the entirety of the distance, the wind about him shifted direction and forced him to the ground. The lightning began to strike...at him! He rolled with the quickness of his Koth to dodge the onslaught and rolled into the feet of another human. It must have been the last Spirit wielder.

The Spirit wielder was caught off guard. A normal human would not have been able to roll out of the pinning that he had accomplished, let alone into him, and so he fell onto his rear into the squishy, wet grass. Dainn noticed the hold of the winds release him and took the opportunity to push over and straddle the fallen man. He felt the slight warmth of the tattoo to un-fuddle the man's mind light up on his thigh. The fog was cleared from his opponent's mind, but the man had still awakened to being pinned by a stranger with iron fists on his hands, so he immediately began to fight back with physical blows that Dainn parried as softly as he could.

The blonde Spirit wielder came from behind and grabbed the man by his shoulders. She spoke to him reassuringly in a voice that was lost to Dainn in the storm. It had the intended effect though, and the man relinquished his struggle and turned his attention to the greater foe.

Rosco was on the creature's back, striping the massive beast's shoulders and upper arms with his swords. Fur and blood were flying everywhere. Grymm kept the creature's attention focused away from the others with the huge two-handed sword that he brandished. Dainn saw one of Lancet's arrows hit an eye of the ravaged creature and took the opening to speed over as fast as he could, launch off the ground to the stomach of the creature, and then spring once more to hit Ramanatra in the jaw with his fists. The blow knocked the creature over with its belly in the air. Grymm was on top of the creature and burying his sword into the creature's chest with Rosco shortly behind him. With three swords in its chest, an arrow in its eye, and an untold amount of other damage taken, the creature stopped breathing on the battlefield. The surrounding storm slowly began to die down with the source of its magic removed. Specks of blue sky could be seen peeking through the dismal darkness of the storm with streaks of sunshine penetrating the gloom with glowing hope.

As it was with many battle trials, Dainn felt himself begin to disappear. His body was flickering in and out of existence. He knew what was happening. He was going back to the portal room now that they had succeeded. A part of him wanted to talk more with the Spirit wielders, but that was not meant to be. They were from a different time, and as Dainn knew, a different planet. Once he returned, he would talk with Scilla. He would see if any of these Spirit wielders were mentioned in detail with the history of this battle to satisfy his curiosity. For now, he had other duties to attend to once they materialized back into the cave of portals. He did the best thing he could think of in the limited time he had. He glanced over at the closer Spirit wielder, the blonde woman, and bowed deeply in gratitude before completely disappearing from that realm.

Chapter 16

The late afternoon sun beat down on Dainn's skin as he approached the Elder's Circle. The palms of his hands were sweating from a combination of sun exposure and nerves when he presented himself at the entrance doors and was admitted. Once inside, the strange magic of the area kept it cool beneath the shade of the leafy palm trees. The relaxing, smoky smell of ylang-ylang and lavender incense came from thin twirls of smoke rising from the mouths of white, coiled snake pots outside each of the elder's stucco huts that surrounded the extinguished fire pit.

This trip to the Elder's Circle was different from the many others Dainn had made in the past. He was not requesting access to a trial, but he was going to be participating in a conversation with the Elders. They had invited him and his friends over for afternoon tea. This was unheard of amongst the Ignet, but so was the return of those lost in the trials. Never in the recorded history of the Ignet had someone who had fallen in a trial returned.

It had been a joyous reunion for Dainn and Lancet when they returned to the cave of portals with their previously lost friends. Elasche had still been waiting when they materialized from the portal, and she gasped with awe and excitement as three additional people rolled out with them. Dainn and Lancet had embraced and hurrahed their old comrades, elaborating on how wonderful it was to have them back. Lancet had even given Denna a loving kiss on the forehead amidst the others causing her to blush fiercely.

Denna, Rosco, and Grymm had contrarily seemed incredibly confused by all the commotion. After a brief discussion, it became apparent that none of them recalled failing the trial previously, and it was noticed that their bodies and minds were preserved exactly as they were almost 20 years ago when they were first trapped in the portal while Krael and the people residing on it had aged without them. Time waited for no one.

Denna had broken into tears when introduced to Elasche, the princess that she had been assigned to protect as an Ignet. The last time Denna had seen her, Elasche had been a young child who was just starting to toddle across the floor. She cupped the girl's cheek in her hand and looked into her eyes stating how they were close enough in age that they could be sisters now. Elasche had embraced her and told her how well Dainn had taken care of her in the meantime as Denna's tears wet her white garb.

The initial reunion was over, and the three lost companions had spent some time getting reacquainted with the world as it existed now. Finding all that had passed and been created without them, sharing as many tears as there were smiles. They were all at the Elder's Circle presently, sitting cross-legged on the straw mats provided to them. Along with the Ignet, Scilla had been granted a special invitation since she was the one who had known the history of the battles against the splicers of Ghaleon's time well enough to rescue the trapped Ignet.

The tea had been sitting in front of each straw mat at the perfect sipping temperature upon their arrival. The teacups were white with golden snakes weaving across them. One of the snake's bodies was made into the teacup's handle. Small portions of honey and milk were placed on a side plate for sweetening if they desired. A golden snake wound its way around the perimeter of the saucers matching the delicate cups.

The elders were sitting in their usual places on straw mats across the firepit. Their eyes were closed, unmoving heads tilted downwards. They sat silently, until in a synchronized motion they all looked up to the visiting group. "Welcome," the voice of the elder sitting in the front, center greeted them with a warm smile. "How is the tea? We hope you find it to your liking."

The visiting group shot Dainn sidelong glances that he could feel without seeing, imploring him to take the lead and respond, "It is very delicious, honored one. We thank you for the hospitality that you so humbly grant us who are barely worthy of your presence."

"Rubbish, young Ignet," the elder responded, waving off Dainn's words with a sweep of his hand. He stood up and bowed his head slightly toward Dainn, "Today, the honor is ours to be learning from you. Please, enlighten us on how you scratched the surface of the mysteries enshrouding the portals."

Dainn nodded toward Scilla to give her proper credit, "It is Scilla's vast knowledge of history that made this possible. While we were visiting Tendyis to track down her brother, she told me the story of an old battlefield behind her hometown. That old battlefield looked exactly like the one where we had failed our trail. She knew that the battle had been won against the splicer, Ramanatra, and that the Ignet had joined forces with the Spirit users to defeat him. The mistake we had made in the trial was thinking that everyone there was our enemy. We should have done more research and recreated the historic event that was being modeled."

Dainn's matter-of-fact voice switched into a more inquisitive tone, "Does this mean that all of the portals are linked to historic events, respected elder?"

The elder doing the talking had been intently listening while pacing back and forth with his hands folded behind his back. He shook his head in response to Dainn's question. "It means at least *some* of the portals are linked to events in history. A sample size of one is not conclusive, but we should investigate. The implications of what has happened here reach far beyond that finding. Expand your mind, Dainn. If history can be stored for eons within the portals and you can bring your friends back in pristine condition from many years ago, what else could happen?"

Dainn heard Scilla gasp audibly, coughing slightly on her tea, clearly understanding the implications that the elder was hinting at. "The splicers..." she choked out in between sputters of tea.

Dainn's eyes widened as he looked back to the elder, "Is she right? Could the splicers or other abominations that we encounter within the portals somehow substantiate into reality? The portals are made of flarium. Maybe only Ignet can enter them freely since that rock is connected to our Koth?"

The elder locked eyes with Dainn, "We cannot discard the possibility of the splicers or other beings traversing the portals without proper research, but your theory on flarium gating the user to having opened their Koth is a good one that should be investigated. This is an old magic. The portals were created even before we elders. We have hints of old magic here, but it is nothing compared to what has been lost over the millennia." The elder paused thoughtfully before continuing and dropped Dainn's gaze to pace again, "Maybe 'lost' is not the right word, but possibly 'evolved'. What we do today has evolved in ways that allowed beings to survive the circumstances that they encountered. Sometimes for better, sometimes for worse."

"You may have noticed that we elders look the same each time you see us. This knowledge is to remain within this group, but we have far exceeded what is considered a general life expectancy. What you see of us here are holograms of ourselves." The elder moved his hand through Dainn's arm to prove this point as he spoke, and Dainn felt nothing but bafflement. "Our bodies live stagnant inside those huts, housed in small portals maintaining our consciousness and brains while our corporeal limbs slumber. We convene with our minds and have essentially become one big brain trust. We have found that voices unaccompanied by bodies do not settle well with most people, nor does direct telepathy, so we have created this visual ruse to make social encounters more comfortable. My thoughts are seen and heard by all my brethren here, and we think and decide as one. We generally choose to speak together as a group when addressing supplicants for dramatics. We could just as easily speak through one of us as we do now." The elder shrugged before moving back to his straw mat away from Dainn.

"When we decided to band together like this, we thought that we were committing forever. Exchanging our bodily enjoyments for eternal life and preservation of knowledge. We wonder now, if we left our portals, would we be the same as we were when we first entered, just like your friends who have rejoined us?" The elder gestured to Denna, Grymm, and Rosco, inspecting them before continuing, "Would we be able to live through our entire remaining mortal lives before experiencing a true death? Ah… those are matters of discussion for another day. Young Ignet, you have opened many questions for old minds that already contain a vast repository of knowledge. For today, we wish for all the Ignet here to study what they can of the portals, taking into consideration what ones contain potentially dangerous creatures to be unleashed. Try to connect those to any historical events, and we here will think about ways to contain them with the magics that we possess. Also, try to find where other Ignet may have been stranded over the years. We may be able to bring them home too."

Dainn responded, "Yes, sir. We will. If I may ask, if you are all holograms and cannot leave your huts, how did you make this tea?"

A tooth-bearing grin spread across the elder's face, "No reason to reveal *all* our secrets to you today but do plan on returning for similar discussions on your research findings. Maybe as you learn more about the portals, you shall learn more about us elders."

***

Ghaleon witnessed the conversation from above and let himself chuckle at the Ignet elders. He had known a few of them while they had all been alive in the usual way. They were good people. Sometimes he wondered if he should have joined them in their portal prisons. Were they not being better guides to the mortal world than he was? Even in death, he always questioned the choice that he had begged the Greatest Spirit for. No matter how much good in his life he had accomplished, there was always another path to consider. There was always something more that he thought he could have done, and no way to know the possible results of the paths not taken.

He sighed to himself, collecting his thoughts. The elders were right. They needed to keep the memories of any splicers trapped inside those portals. The worlds were still succumbing to the evil remnants that the last splicers left behind, as shown by Sonu, Kaitzen, and countless others with twisted hearts. Ghaleon had destroyed all the splicers that he was aware of in his lifetime as Spirit Master. Mory had destroyed at least two creatures that had been in the process of absorbing hatred and evil before morphing into full-fledged splicers. One on Tendyis recently, and one on Krael last year. Who knew how many more were growing, sprinkled across the universe?

Sonu could possibly help with that. Maybe he could find a way to search other planets in other galaxies for growing splicers and report back to Mory. Purging one planet or one solar system or one galaxy was not enough when splicers could travel across the void of space so easily. A great weight fell upon Ghaleon, that search would be an endless task for Sonu, condemning him to an eternity of the half-death in which he was currently trapped. The universe was just so large. He was Ghaleon. He would find a way, but that was a task for another day. For now, there were no full-fledged splicers roaming the galaxies, so the best medicine would be to spread love, joy, and kindness to help heal those in pain and to minimize the possible growth of any more splicers. Without feeding off evil emittances, any emergent splicers could not fully mature.

***

The suns had sunken below the horizon, giving way to a star-speckled night sky by the time everyone had left the Elder's Circle. Scilla removed her boots to walk barefoot across the cool night sand, something that she never could have done during the heat of the day. The feeling of the sand squishing between her toes was therapeutic to her.

Before leaving Tendyis, Miran had taken a liking to Nico and offered to let him stay with him. That was refreshing since Scilla wasn't sure if the young groundling was ready to leave his home planet yet. There was still so much for him to explore and grow with on Tendyis. Miran had made it very clear to Scilla that he would love to see her again once she had everything straightened out on Krael, and he elicited a promise out of her to return to tell him her story. Scilla wasn't quite sure what to think about Miran yet. He had locked her in a meat cellar upon their first meeting, but he seemed to have a good heart and was trying to do the right thing. If anything, it gave her a reason to see her home planet once more.

Since returning to Krael, everything seemed to happen at once. Scilla was beyond thankful that she had her future sight back thanks to returning with a bag stuffed full of clarum. She had found Kaitzen alive by walking the paths of the future and encountering him down various possible paths. Relief had flooded her, accompanied by guilt. His survival not only meant that Scilla still had a chance to save him, but it also meant that people on Krael were suffering because of his actions. Scilla needed to act fast to contain him before he could spread his evil anymore.

As Sonu had predicted, Kaitzen was stirring up trouble. The kind of trouble that he had selected was assembling an army to attack the Saliek and Arbore. He was quite angry about being pushed through the portal on Tendyis without Ghaleon's cloak and wanted to get revenge on the ones he had seen on Tendyis. It was a predictable move to even those who weren't seers based on his previous behavior. Conveniently, the Saliek camp and Arbore were very close to each other, and he had sent rather dramatic threats to Regithal -the Saliek'an- and Kylie's blood father -the king of Arbore. Neither man would generally stir to threats, but an army of creatures had slowly been amassing outside the mountain pass to Arbore. Since then, Regithal and the king had been working together to ready their armies to protect Arbore.

Kaitzen had been growing his army by questionable means, as always. There were an increasing number of tales of attacks on defenseless citizens to gather followers or supplies since his return to Krael. He would use his creatures or magic from his relics to quickly demolish his adversaries since his favorite kind of battle was one with the odds in his favor. This was creating mistrust and fear among those who did not manifest any magical traits. They were not fond of being bullied by someone more powerful than them whom they were incapable of resisting in non-magical ways.

Rumors surrounding the formation of a syndicate containing those against all magic users were beginning to become more prevalent. They called themselves the Syn. Scilla's premonitions warned her of the possible danger that they presented if they were allowed to grow in strength. The smothering of Kaitzen's influence quickly was necessary to decrease problematic affairs of the future.

***

A few days prior…

A pre-teen boy with brown hair carried a pole across his back balancing a bucket of water on one end and a bucket of chicken feed on the other. One of Jasper's chores was to care for the chickens that the traveling health clinic that he lived with relied upon for eggs. His father was a practiced surgeon who used non-magical means to cure ailments. He had gathered a moderately sized medical team that traveled from city to city in horse-drawn wagons administering their professions. There were many out there who had superstitions or did not completely trust medical mending of magical means, so his father had quite a large clientele across the cities that he traversed between. Some radicals would even go as far as tracking their band down mid-travel for life-critical treatment rather than seek the help of a magically aided healer in their towns.

Jasper was learning healing skills from his father. His older sister was already a talented nurse whom his father took as an aid into any surgery that he was completing. Jasper was currently mastering how to make medicines from various wild herbs that they came across. He saw the purple leaves of marloom sprouting across from where the rolling chicken coop had been set for the evening. He knew that collecting the marloom for his father would make him very happy since marloom was a potent pain-killing herb that he used frequently on his patients.

Jasper scattered the chicken feed on the ground outside and poured the water into the trough inside the chicken coop. While the chickens pecked around the ground, he stuffed a large amount of the marloom into his pockets, eager for his father's praise. While crouched in the marloom bunches, he heard something whistle over his head followed by a loud crackling as a lightning bolt shredded one of the wagons throwing splinters of shattered wood in all directions. He heard cries of pain when the wood must have struck a person. Then another whistle across the camp came, and a different wagon erupted into flames.

People were racing out of their wagons and shooing their children into hiding places wherever they could find them. Flames crept from wagon to wagon causing the horses to flee with wild eyes while tossing their manes. Random shrieks pierced Jasper's ears from across the camp. Lighting was raining down upon them now, and devastation wrecked on every corner. The chickens had all run back into their coop, leaving the feed behind. Utter chaos reigned.

Jasper was scared. He wanted to find his father. He ran back toward their wagon and saw far too many horrors along the way for his young mind to comprehend. He knew the injuries that he witnessed were bad, sometimes very bad, based on living so close to the medical world, but coping with death was not something that his father had tainted his young mind with yet. He flung open the door to their wagon and saw a scurgel had ripped the side of the wagon off and held his father by the neck. His sister was flung against the wall. She wasn't moving. Jasper froze, hands trembling.

"The medical supplies, where are they!" the scurgel demanded. "We are confiscating them."

"They are probably in one of the wagons that you've already destroyed," his father responded with an ornery kick to his voice.

The scurgel swung him unhappily back and forth, and Jasper saw his father's head shake viciously.

"LIES!" the scurgel screamed, getting drops of mucus-like spittle onto his father's face. "They are here in this wagon." Jasper's father said nothing and just looked back at the scurgel, straight into its eyes.

Jasper saw the scurgel's focus flick toward him, and then something made a multitude of surgical instruments clang together on a desk before levitating and flying over to Jasper. They all pointed threateningly at his neck being held by nothing but thin air. Jasper started whimpering, "Daddy, help me."

"NO!" screamed Jasper's father.

"Medical supplies, *now*, or the boy gets it." The scurgel set his father down with the ultimatum to consider. The man hurried to a trap door that was set in the corner of the wagon. He pulled out a locked metal box and unlocked it with a key around his neck that had been tucked into his shirt. He walked over to the scurgel, proffering his medical prizes, and finally saw the man that Jasper had already noticed with red glowing eyes standing behind the scurgel. It was the man who was magically threatening Jasper's life with the surgical instruments. Jasper's father quivered with anger and anxiety as he presented the box, open, to the scurgel.

Inside that box were some of his most precious possessions concocted of the rarest herbs. These were the medications that could work magic without being magical. In this instance, the magic they would work would be saving Jasper's life at the cost of the countless others that could have been saved at his father's hand with the medicines inside that box. Jasper knew that. Jasper had been studying how to make those medicines.

"Daddy, don't do it. It's okay," Jasper said, but it was too late. The scurgel snatched the box away, and the surgical tools clamored to the floor surrounding Jasper. The red-eyed Spirit user turned away, and the carnage on the traveling medical team halted.

Jasper ran to his father's open arms, and he felt his father's tears wetting his shirt. "It'll be okay Daddy. We will make it okay," Jasper said, mimicking what he had heard his father say to others before when he was trying to comfort them. At that, his father hugged him tighter before letting go and grasping Jasper's chin in his hands to studiously look over his face.

"I found these for you, Daddy!" Jasper offered, trying to make his father smile again as he handed him the marloom that was scrunched up from his pockets. Smile his father did at Jasper.

"Thank you, son. This is just what we need," his father said, taking the herbs and going over to investigate Jasper's sister's situation. "Jasper, you remember the person who was here earlier today, delivering herbs and requesting services?"

"Yes," Jasper acknowledged remembering the hooded character since they were particularly strange looking.

"Good," His father's next words were slightly stammered, "If anything more happens here, like it did today, I want you to run away from this camp. Don't look for me, just run. I'll know where to find you. Run to Arbore, no matter how far we are away. I want you to *run to Arbore* and ask for Laurel of the Syn. I had been hesitating to join them, but after this attack today, I feel like we have no other choice. They will take care of you if…anything else happens. You know, anything else like today."

Jasper nodded, "I will."

"Promise me, Jasper. Promise me that you'll run if this happens again," his father insisted.

"I promise, Daddy. I will run."

"Good, lad. Now go check on those chickens while I tend to Sissy, they must be terrified too. Maybe it scared a good egg or two out of them, eh?" his father shooed Jasper away as he turned his attention to Sissy.

Jasper looked back over his shoulder as he was leaving the wagon. He saw his father go into another trap door on the floor of the wagon and pull out another box. His father saw him peeking, and he gave Jasper a wink and a smile. Jasper realized then that maybe the medicine wasn't all gone. He had a smart Daddy.

Chapter 17

The Golden Plains at the foot of the Sentinel mountains, beyond the crags of the pass carved through Sentinel's Gate that led into Arbore, spread on for as far as the eye could see. In the distance, they melted into the evening sky riddled with the pinks, yellows, and blues of the setting suns. It was ordinarily a vast, open sea of wheat-colored waves in this late autumn season, but the usual peace was disrupted by the chaos of Kaitzen's compiled army of underlings that hadn't forsaken him since the time of his departure over a year ago. The number of followers that he had maintained was impressive and spread across many sentient species of Krael. Knowledge of the future was a pretty hefty bargaining tool that he held. They all looked vicious, blood-thirsty, and hinted at the verge of insanity in certain cases. Kaitzen had scraped the bottom of the moral barrel across Krael and came out with a savage masterpiece for his army.

Each type of creature had its own way of readying themselves for the imminent battle. Tiny-looking firelings bounced up and down with their tribal beaded necklaces and earrings clacking to a menacing rhythm. Traitor humans with sneers on their faces and malicious glares in their eyes were wiping down their weapons and sizing up their human counterparts across the field. Towering scurgels were flexing their muscles at each other, blood vessels nearly ripping through their flesh as they screamed toward the skies. Crafty grafters were working on creating sticky traps in various locations across the battlefield to slow incoming attackers.

Each of them looked menacing in their own regard, but each group was separated. There would be little collaboration between the races of Kaitzen's army.

The Saliek and Arbore armies had gathered at the very edge of the mountains, immediately outside the passage to Arbore. The Sentinels, with their patchwork of autumn reds and golds, protected their flank and provided a gorgeous backdrop to what would likely soon become a field of carnage. Contrary to Kaitzen's army, their ranks were orderly, and their leaders had their squadrons well-trained and organized.

Saliek'an Regithal looked regal, positioned at the front of the army atop his pegasus, Valor, staring into the depths of the enemy lines, eyes fixated on discerning any notable activities or patterns. His black Saliek cloak waved behind him slightly as the chilly breeze played with the cloth and picked up loose strands of his blue Spirit-streaked, black hair. Valor's bright white blaze down his nose was crossed with stray wisps of his pure black mane and tufts of his tail flew haphazardly as the breeze blew through. Regithal's swept-back cloak revealed his broadsword affixed to his side with magnificent gems on its hilt of emerald, sapphire, and diamond sparkling in the sunlight. Bright splashes of color against his otherwise black ensemble. He very much looked like a general who would intimidate the hearts of his enemies.

Next to him sat Zhannah on her grey, dappled pegasus, Storm. Her blonde hair, enhanced by her yellow Spirit color, was pulled back into her customary battle braid and gleamed like a shiny ribbon in the sunlight. Her dual swords were sheathed, crossed along her back, ready for whatever may come. Her face was set in a determined gaze, and it looked as though she knew that she would not fail her friends this day. The rest of the Saliek gathered behind them, flying purple banners emblazoned with a white rearing pegasus throughout the ranks. Some were mounted on their pegasi.

Others were afoot. All of them sported their black cloaks and glowing, colorful eyes. It had been many years since the Saliek had been a part of a head-to-head battle that Kaitzen was now forcing, but they were well-trained, experienced, and ever-ready for the turmoil.

Behind the Saliek was the army of Arbore led by their king, Kylie's blood father. That army was full of the non-Spirit user residents of Arbore, and they were all adorned in shiny metallic armor. Their helms covered their faces completely with small, slanted slits where their eyes should be, and longer vertical slits stitched along their mouth. Horns curled out of the sides of the helmets and from atop the shields carried by some of them. Their banner was a golden dragon on an emerald backdrop, and their armor mimicked the beast's traits when feasible. The king had made sure that supply lines would run the gorge back to Arbore to keep the armies maintained as needed.

Kylie was clustered in the Saliek army ranks with Scilla, Mory, Anik, Dainn, Denna, and Elasche. Denna had refused to be left behind in Mahashta since, in her mind, Elasche was still her's to protect. No one had relieved her from that duty, even if Dainn had stepped in while she was sequestered away within the portal. Elasche and Dainn were not about to turn her away. She was as capable, if not more capable, than them in battle and had no other responsibilities at home holding her back since she so recently returned from supposed death. Her braided bear ears looked far too adorable for the battlefield, but that was her style. She swore it was functional as well as fashionable.

Kylie, Mory, Scilla, and Anik were all mounted on their respective pegasi, while Dainn, Denna, and Elasche were on foot. They had been offered to borrow pegasi to ride, but none of them had been comfortable battling from on top of a mount. They had been trained as ground soldiers. They would stay with the main forces of the army to distract them while Kylie, Mory, Anik, and Scilla would be trying to isolate Kaitzen. Scilla was still convinced that she could reason with him one-on-one, but Regithal had made it clear to her and the others what she must do if she failed. His extermination would be for the good of the rest of Krael.

Kylie felt extremely nervous, and her hands were beginning to clam up which would make wielding her daggers tricky. She knew that she was capable of fighting and had done it in the past, but not in a full-fledged battle with hundreds or maybe even thousands of participants on the battlefield. She saw Anik and Bandit ahead of her, looking cool, calm, and collected. It seemed as though he did this sort of thing every day. He didn't look phased in the slightest. In fact, he almost looked excited as he rubbed Bandit's neck and snuck her a blapple from his saddle bag. Scilla was nearby with her eyes closed on top of her big bay, Shadow. Kylie had seen that demeanor worn by Scilla before, and she knew that she was forcefully tracing the paths of the future. She was likely trying to figure out where she could find Kaitzen and how she would most likely be able to turn him back to a good cause.

Mory was behind her, sitting tall and silent upon his white Knight wearing all three of Ghaleon's artifacts for all to see. Soldiers in the army ranks tried not to stare at the picturesque, renowned Spirit Master, but their sidelong glances gave them away. They were whispering amongst themselves, probably speculating on why he wasn't at the front of the charge, but he ignored them well. They had no way of knowing his true purpose back here, and it was best that they didn't. Kylie silently wondered if Mory should address those near him, to give them strength and courage for the upcoming battle. Then she realized that he must be nervous too. He doesn't want to spread his own fear, so his presence would have to be enough. She understood that. She knew that she could not trust her own words from wavering in this situation.

Kylie turned forward and patted Starshine's golden neck. She whispered the encouraging words that she felt she needed to hear herself into the pegasus' ears in an attempt to soothe her own growing anxiety. Sometimes comforting others in your own time of need helped you to cope with your own emotions. As Kylie was losing the battle to her overwhelming fear, she felt Mory's comforting hand on her shoulder. He had walked Knight over to her and Starshine, and he began rubbing her back.

"Don't worry, golden one, we won't be here for long. You remember the plan. When Regithal gives the 'go' to charge after the first sun has set, we will fly away in the chaos as opposed to charging in with the armies. We will find Kaitzen from above with Scilla's help and take him on separately. With any luck, it will be four against one. You can't scoff at those odds!"

Kylie couldn't help but crack a smile. Mory always knew what to say to help her through a difficult situation. She put her hand on top of one of his that were on her shoulders, met his eyes, and said, "Thank you." He smiled his goofy smile in response, and they sat in companionable silence while watching the puffs of clouds bathe in the brightly painted sky until Regithal let Kylie know over their mental connection that he had given the order to charge.

In a synchronized movement, pegasi flew into the air, and men and women ran forward toward Kaitzen's army with loud yells, shrill shrieks, and weapons clanking. Scilla held her arm up in a 'hold' position to signal to her small group to wait. She waited until the skies filled with a decent amount of Saliek riders before letting her hand drop and announcing, "We fly!"

The four of them flew close to one another in a diamond formation near the side edge of the battlefield, as far from the center as they could get themselves, while still looking to be a part of the charge. Scilla led, Anik guarded their rear, and Kylie and Mory flew side-by-side in between them.

Upon hitting the sky, enemy archers turned their sights on them. Anik used the winds to deflect the flying arrows forcing them to fall harmlessly, fletching down, onto the battlefield below.

Even though they had let others go before them, it didn't take long before an enemy wyvern-looking creature sighted them and started flying in their direction. While Anik continued to take care of the arrows, Mory turned his attention toward the wyvern. It began to sink toward the ground. It looked as though the effort to create the upward motion in its flap to keep airborne was getting more and more difficult. "Gravity can really weigh you down!" Mory shouted to the creature as it slowly descended below the level at which the group was flying. Kylie saw another one coming at them that happened to shoot something out of its mouth. She reformed the clouds into a sphere around them and solidified them into an ice shield blocking the projectile before it hit the group. Mory worked his gravity trick again with that wyvern while Kylie maintained the ice shield around them as they flew through the sky. They continued working in this repeating algorithm for a while before Kylie realized how strained she was feeling. The others must feel it too.

"Scilla, have you found him yet?" Kylie shouted above the clatter of projectiles on the shifting ice shield.

"Almost there…" Scilla replied while gently trying to encourage Shadow to fly faster. He was the eldest pegasus of the group, and his speed was their limiting factor. Kylie saw that he was already dripping in sweat and knew Scilla wouldn't be getting much more out of him.

"Watch out!" Mory screamed too late as a wyvern who had escaped his gravity amplification rammed up into the ice shield from below physically crashing into the group. The ice shield shattered throwing ice chunks everywhere. The sheer size of the wyvern knocked the four of them out of the sky. The tired pegasi tried to recover, but the best they could do was wrap their wings around their riders before they hit the ground. One of the others must have had something left in them because their impact was softened by a helpful gust of wind. It took all of Kylie's concentration just to hang on.

Kylie was hugging Starshine's neck when they hit, and once the world seemed stable, she finally released her grasp. "Starshine! Are you okay?" she asked with panic in her voice. She felt the pegasus' neck quiver in response with a weak-sounding whinny. Starshine was alive. Kylie rolled off Starshine's back since Starshine had landed on her knees, successfully avoiding pinning Kylie's leg beneath her side. Kylie used her Spirit to heal Starshine's flesh wounds as best as she could. Shadow, with his years of experience, had somehow managed to land on his feet allowing Scilla to dismount before he laid down on the ground to rest. Mory and Knight had been flung up against the mountainside, and although their one side looked a little worse for wear, they were both mostly okay. She saw Anik had not been as fortunate with Bandit though. Bandit had landed on her side, crushing Anik's leg beneath her. Bandit was hurt, but alive. Unfortunately, the girth of her blapple-loving belly was making it impossible for her to get up as her legs flailed uselessly out to the side. Each time she moved, Anik's leg got more crushed causing him to wince and groan. The three of them ran over to calm Bandit and help Anik.

"My leg!" Anik said through clenched teeth. He was obviously in a lot of pain.

"We see," Kylie said, kneeling by Bandit's head trying to soothe her. She put her hands on both of Bandit's cheeks and pulled her own forehead close to the white mask marking across Bandit's eyes before speaking in a soft tone, "Hush now, girl, you're fine. Just a little stuck. You're such a good girl. Such a pretty and patient girl. Let us get you up so we can help Anik." Scilla and Mory had positioned themselves along Bandit's back to roll her up onto her feet by the time Bandit's breathing had slowed into a more relaxed cadence.

Kylie started a countdown once everyone seemed in place, “Are you ready? One…Two…Three!” Mory and Scilla pushed simultaneously, and Bandit shifted her weight to help. After large amounts of grunting from all involved, Bandit was rolled back onto her feet, and Anik’s leg was freed.

“Thank you,” he said while clutching his leg. Bandit lowered her head down to him, snuffling in apology, and looked up at the rest of them to see if they could help her disabled rider. “I can heal the flesh wounds,” Anik said while they saw the worst of the gashes knit themselves together, “I studied up a little on healing since our battles last year, but I didn’t learn enough about bone structure to be able to put my leg’s bone back together.”

Kylie wished that Elasche was here right now, but no amount of wishing would make that true. She was tired, but not completely spent. She had read books about how bones were meant to be shaped, and she knew Mory had too while studying under Scilla. They could do this. Mory must have thought the same thing.

Mory spoke up, “Scilla, you continue to save your energy for Kaitzen. Kylie and I will mend Anik enough so he can move again.” Mory turned to Anik, “We’ve not done this before, so it may not be perfect. Elasche, or someone better trained in healing, may have to complete the job later. Are you okay with us continuing?”

“Yes, of course! I trust you will help some. It can’t get much worse than this,” Anik responded eagerly.

Mory turned to Kylie, “I will set the bone, you mend the muscles around it to hold it in place.”

Kylie nodded and closed her eyes to better remember the muscle structure of human legs.

“Wait,” Mory said reaching out to hold her arm, “Let me fix the bone first, then you mend the muscle. I’ll start from the thigh and go down.” She nodded.

Anik started groaning as Mory began his work, and he took a chunk of cloth from his cloak and stuffed it into his own mouth for something to bite down on while they healed him. Kylie waited a few minutes before starting to follow down the leg. She could see the bones realigning and stitching themselves back into proper placement through Anik's skin. The leg rounded back into a more recognizable shape as Mory moved down the leg. By the time they finished, Anik was gasping and spat out the well-chewed piece of his cloak while he inspected their work.

"Wow! I'm impressed," Anik said as he admired their handy work on his leg. He tried to stand but was a bit wobbly. It hurt him to put all his weight on the mended leg. Kylie saw this and handed him a knobby branch that she had found nearby for him to use as a walking stick in the near term. "Thank you, guys. Seriously, I wouldn't know what to do without you. You know, except lay on the ground screaming in pain and regretting all the extra blapples that I snuck to Bandit." Bandit snorted indignantly at the comment but continued to headbutt Anik as he scratched her forehead lovingly.

"No worries. You would do the same for any of us," Mory responded, patting Anik on the back. Then he put on his teasing voice to lighten the situation, "Speaking of which, you are an absolutely brilliant battle wizard, but may I suggest you study healing a bit more in-depth upon your return? I mean, how can you return the favor if you've got your head wrapped around all this fancy elemental magic?" Mory winked to emphasize the point that he was kidding, and Anik took the stick that Kylie had given him and poked it at Mory, lightly tapping him in mock battle movements, as they started laughing together.

Now that the situation had settled down, Kylie started to take in the area around their landing ground. They had fallen far on one of the sides of the battlefield where the mountains still crept out onto the plains. She noted how high up they were when she walked over to the edge of the precipice and looked down its sheer, rocky face. A pile of pebbles disturbed by her footsteps clattered and clicked in a stirring of dust. The scree bounced and rolled off the ledge, falling until she could no longer see them. She felt a moment of vertigo watching their descent and quickly stepped back to allow the dizziness to pass before scanning the raging battle on the plains below.

The suns had set completely now, and darkness obscured the fighting. The glow of the eyes of the spirited could be seen as colorful pinpricks moving about the sea of darkness. She cocked her head toward the heavens and noted the similarity to the stars of the night sky. The stars weren't as colorful as the eyes of the spirited, but they had a certain twinkle to them that could not be replicated by a mortal being. She could hear them calling to her with clarity in the night. The time she would need them is soon. That is what they told her. Kylie still had not figured out how to share their strength with others. That disappointed her greatly. She didn't want to let anyone down when they needed her. She hoped that she would figure it out quickly. In her exhaustion, she breathed in deeply for a sigh, and she suddenly felt her Spirit re-invigorated. The stars had re-filled her. She smiled up at them in thanks.

A maniacal laugh filled the night air. Kylie turned swiftly to see a crazed-looking Kaitzen making his way down a narrow, curving mountain path. Two fully armored humans lead the way down toward the group, and Kylie could hear more footfalls behind them. Before more could come into sight, an avalanche occurred precisely blocking the rest of the mountain path. Other than Kaitzen and the two humans leading him, one scurgel had been on the side of the wreckage nearest to their group. Anik smiled to himself while leaning on both of his hands folded over the top of his new walking staff before proclaiming, "It will take months to clear that rubble away, Kaitzen. Your troops are diminished to what you have with you now. No others can reach you."

"Silly, silly, boy," Kaitzen shook his head, and words dripping with condescension continued to pour out of his mouth, "Had I wanted to engage you in battle, I would have snuck up on you and attacked. I only wish to speak to my dear sister here."

"I am here Kaitzen. Leave the others alone," Scilla put herself in between Kaitzen and the rest of the group, "Of what do you wish to speak?"

Kaitzen forcefully pushed his way in front of his cronies and looked Scilla in the eyes. Kylie noticed that even though they were twins and their overall looks were similar, they were not identical in all ways. Scilla's eyes held the glow of a pale lavender Spirit, whereas Kaitzen's did not, and Scilla's features were slightly less pointy and sharp than those of Kaitzen's. What stood out the most was their demeanors. Scilla portrayed confidence and strength, whereas Kaitzen was cocky and prideful.

"Join me," he said simply and reached his hand out to hers. When Scilla didn't respond, he added, "No others have the gift of foresight on Krael. We could rule them. They would come to us with their issues, and we could administer our help as we desired. No one could bully us ever again."

Scilla held her ground, hands at her sides, as she responded, "We can help them without ruling over them, Kaitzen, as I do now. Put a halt to this frivolous battle. You have me here now. This is what you wanted. Let there be no more dying tonight."

The craze in Kaitzen's eyes flared, "Oh no, dear sister," he hissed, "It is not just you that I wanted. It is ALL of Krael. You will help me accomplish that. We can do this together. We can control this entire planet of pitiful creatures! Watch me. I'll show you."

Kaitzen turned to the scurgel behind him and whispered something in its ear. Without hesitation, the creature leaped from the rocky ledge.

"NO!" Scilla screamed, but she was powerless to stop what had just occurred. She never would have imagined that a creature would so willingly jump to its death at the command of one man, so she hadn't been ready to stop him. Kylie ran to the edge and did her best to slow the fall of the creature. It was hard to see, so she did her work by feel. She hoped that she was successful.

"You see," Kaitzen said as if nothing out of the ordinary had just happened, "I told him that he would fly if he jumped. That was one of his greatest dreams, to soar above the clouds and see the world from on high. I promised him long ago that I would fulfill that dream for him. I showed it to him in a vision as proof with help from one of my handy-dandy artifacts, and I have just kept that side of my bargain with him." Kaitzen paused to tilt his head back and laugh hysterically before continuing, "He has seen all he wanted to see on his fall through the clouds, and one of your children tried to save him. He will land safely because of their intervention. I foresaw this. He will thank me later for my generosity. Do you see the power that we could command, Scilla? Can you fathom it?"

Scilla was shaking her head vigorously, "No, Kaitzen, I will absolutely not join you. Especially after that demonstration. You know that is not what the scurgel wanted. You did not gift him what he desired no matter how much your mind twists it. Where is my brother? Where is the shy, curious boy always experimenting and learning?"

Kaitzen responded in a soft, menacing tone, "Why, he's right here, Scilla. I am right here before you. Can't you see me?" He reached out and forcefully grasped her hands this time, so he could not be refused again. For a moment, they stared at each other, until Scilla started to lurch violently in a fit of screams. Kaitzen began his tirade again with anger flooding his voice, "If you will not join me, then I need to take away the power from the only one who can rival me. That person is you, Scilla. This experimenting boy has learned that not only can clarum give us our power, but it can take it away too, under the right circumstances. An ancient artifact from my stash that was believed to have been used in the past to suck souls away from creatures, was actually sucking away their magical powers. Since the properties of clarum include charging and discharging the powers for a seer, if a piece of clarum is near you, your powers will be stored in the rock when sucked away, conveniently there for me to call upon later!"

The look in Kaitzen's eyes was pure evil. He seemed to be enjoying the pain he was causing his sister by taking away her most cherished treasure. Kylie would have no more of this. She turned her face to the stars and asked for their help. She heard the song of their voices grow in loudness until they blanketed her. She felt a hand on one shoulder first, Mory. Then a hand on her other shoulder, Anik.

"We will help you, Kylie," Mory said and then lifted his head toward the skies, "Please, lend us all your strength to get through and save our friend!"

Anik echoed his plea as well, "Yes, please help us. We are willing to fight to save her and her powers."

That gesture must have been what the stars were looking for. The others had to acknowledge that they wanted the strength of the stars before it was shared with them as well as Kylie. They needed to all acknowledge the need for help.

The light of the stars that was centered on Kylie grew around Mory and Anik before blossoming out into a sphere that encompassed everyone on the mountain ledge. The men who Kaitzen had brought opened arrow fire upon Kylie, but ghostly Sonu appeared, solidified, and crashed into them before their arrows flew. He held them pinned in place against the mountain with an otherworldly strength while Kylie conversed with the stars. She whispered the names of the stars that she had learned so many nights ago, and the connection solidified. The stars had watched over the past and saved it in their light. A light that they were sending to Kylie. Around her, in the sparkling brightness, a scene played for all to see. A scene of two children being abused by their father in a town that turned a blind eye. A mother being killed. A little girl standing up to the monster while the boy fled. The boy returning and killing the father who was no longer a monster as a girl lay helpless on a couch. And finally, a town condemning the children for something they wanted to bury deep, forget, and tie a bow around.

Kaitzen released Scilla and stepped backward, mouth open, aghast, while watching the light show. Horror reeled through his eyes as memories he had long ago locked away came flooding back into his consciousness. While Kaitzen was stunned by the scene from the stars, he dropped the chunk of clarum that he had presumably been extracting Scilla's powers into. Scilla scrambled desperately over to it, snatched it up, and hugged it close to her breast before pocketing it. The light scene played until the children it depicted were sent through a portal into space and disappeared. Then, the light dissipated, floating back to the heavens in glistening wisps. When the darkness surrounded them once more, it was silent and still, other than the sounds of the distant battle. Everyone was frozen. Kylie felt her heart throbbing in her whole body, not knowing what to do next, but understanding that what she had just seen was a clip from Scilla and Kaitzen's past. Suddenly, Kaitzen ran toward the edge of the rock face and leaped. Scilla stood up and jumped after him.

***

Kaitzen and Scilla grappled one another as they fell. Wind blasted through her hair, making her ears cold and deafening her to anything that was beyond her immediate self. They were twisting as they fell allowing for her Saliek cloak to wrap itself around both of them, binding them together. The rest of the world swirled by in an undistinguishable blur, and the only thing that Scilla could see and hear with clarity was Kaitzen. He struggled frantically to get out of her grasp, but the cloak was wrapped too tightly, and Scilla would not allow for it. He didn't want to be saved. He wanted to perish along with his pain and troubles. He didn't want to go on anymore. He wanted this to be his end.

"Let go of the pain, Kaitzen." Scilla insisted. "It was so long ago. They are gone. We are still here though, and we can make it through. The reason you act as you do, the reason you spit fire with your words and hurt those around you is because you hurt inside. The reason you try to control others is because you couldn't control what happened that day. You are loved Kaitzen. You are forgiven. There is no need to hurt. Let it go. I am here. I love you."

"No!" Kaitzen rebuked. "I don't deserve your kindness. I killed him when he wasn't a monster. He had saved you and was caring for you, and then I killed him."

Scilla attempted to reassure him, "He had killed our mother already, Kaitzen. What you didn't see is that he also tried to kill me that day while you were gone. Something inside stopped him though. Don't become him. Stop your rampage. Learn from his mistakes. Don't let his monster become yours too. Let the goodness inside of him that stayed his hand against me be the goodness that guides you from now on. Find your courage again."

Kaitzen stubbornly replied, "I ran, Scilla, I ran when you saved me. I left you to die. I am a worthless being. You cared enough to save me, and I abandoned you. I have no courage."

Scilla would not back down. She would save her twin, "You came back. You cannot forget that. After all that had happened, you returned to save me. You do have courage."

Kaitzen paused for a moment. Scilla kept going, seeing her words beginning to sink in.

Scilla continued, "I am here now too. I will save you, or rather help you save yourself. You need to let go of the pain for good. Banish the monster that lives within you. Be the Kaitzen that came back to save his sister. Let that be who you are from now on."

Kaitzen tipped his head back and screamed a deep, rough scream, as though a demon inside of him was being let loose into the whipping winds, and Scilla hoped that maybe that was indeed the case. Then, he whispered, "I've done so much wrong though. On multiple planets. How could I ever be truly forgiven? It's best I die now. Let me go, Scilla, please let me go, and let me die so I don't have to face those who I've hurt. You are light, and I am darkness. The worlds need you to banish the darkness with your light."

"No. I will not let you die now." Scilla stood her ground mentally while falling through the sky, staring intently into her twin's eyes as she held him close. She didn't have much longer until they hit the ground now. At least he had stopped struggling as much, so holding onto him was easier. "We will go do our best to make right the wrongs of the past. We may not be able to heal the scars that have formed, but it is possible to try and make sure no others fall to the path that you have walked. Now that you understand why you act as you do, you can control yourself, and help others understand their actions too. Sometimes it takes someone who has already failed, to teach others before they recreate the same failures. The worlds need you to be that teacher, Kaitzen. From one who truly understands what can corrupt a good soul…and, more importantly, one who can best it. You can best it, Kaitzen. I know you can. We can together. You view me as light, but I viewed you as my light growing up. You were brilliant, inventive, and unafraid to break rules for which purposes were dubious. The shadows in your mind only exist because there is a light to cast them. Break free of the obstacle creating the shadow and let your light shine through."

The ground came, and Scilla used her Spirit to allow them both to land softly and alive. Kaitzen was emotionally broken but physically fine from the fall. She held him close as he cried on her shoulder, rocking him soothingly, and consoling him as she would have a child. She would help fill his shattered and cracked soul as best as she could. She knew his pain would not go away immediately, but he seemed willing to let her try to help him now. Scilla didn't need her visions to know that she would succeed. Failure was not an option. Kaitzen would be saved.

Chapter 18

Mount Liriken puffed grey, warped rings of smoke and vapor into the dull sky on Thaer. The slate-colored clouds released the first fall of fluffy snowflakes which began to dot the ground as Scilla was careful not to slip while walking toward the Ancient Archives after running errands in town. She had taken up residence there with Kaitzen. Not only was it good for him to be away from Krael or Tendyis to heal his mind, but it was also good in that he could not be hunted by those that he had angered. Lucky for him, he had not visited Thaer before.

Scilla had brought clarum from her own stash, as well as Kaitzen's, so that their talents would remain strong on Thaer. She did not want to take away his abilities because he would have to learn to live with them. Being a seer was a part of who he was. Zhannah and Regithal had taken to splitting their time between their house on Thaer and at the Saliek camp on Krael to keep Scilla company as she tended to her brother.

Scilla had her hands full with Kaitzen. He teetered on the brink of insanity daily. The evil had chewed up his mind and corrupted it into confusion. The pain would be too much on some days, but on others, he could live a semi-normal life. He was all over the place. A fractured mosaic of feelings, fruitlessly trying to fit himself together. Content, free, confused, lonely, devastated, euphoric, wild, and tortured by memories of the past. Kaitzen was trying on fragments of his new life and piecing them together as best as he could, but he frequently stumbled along the way.

Life is a different place for those in mental or emotional pain. It wobbles on a different axis, at a different speed, lacking any general order or consistency. Time skips backward and forwards fleetingly. They may go through thousands of micro-emotions a day, flailing, trying to figure out how to get through. Moments of strength, independence, and rebellion are intricately woven together with grief, paralyzing vulnerability, and hopelessness. Imagining the future might take them on a detour back to the past and then their world crumbles again. Being around them requires a person with an incredible amount of patience and love in their heart who refuses to give up on them.

Scilla was determined to be that person for Kaitzen. She had been in that kind of pain before when she had lost Andolin, though she had not taken her feelings out on others in society as Kaitzen had done. Zhannah had been there for Scilla in her darkest hours. She would pay the good deed forward to Kaitzen. She could almost feel Andolin's warm breath on her neck now as he pulled her close to tell her how proud he was of her, but that must have just been a breeze from the warm innards of the nearby volcano.

She looked up at the sculptures on the brilliant blue roof atop the black stone building of the Ancient Archives and smiled. She knew her history. The sculptures represented the factions of humans that had banded together at the time of Ghaleon to fight the splicers. The pegasus represented the Spirited Saliek. The dragon represented the magic-less ones. The snake represented the Koth-gifted Ignet. Finally, the fish represented a clan of folk that resided on Blaet who had made the ultimate sacrifice. Their city had been proudly constructed near a beautiful waterfall, but while most of their population was away supporting Ghaleon's efforts, a splicer had sunk their sparsely defended city into the depths of a lake, cursing those who remained to be trapped in fins, just as their banners portrayed. They were cursed to live on as merfolk with no memories of their past. She had been reminded of them earlier when Mory, Kylie, and Anik had visited their sunken city, unintentionally, on Blaet.

She neared the double doors of the entrance and pushed open the demon-faced one. That door portrayed one of the many splicers that fell to Ghaleon's great sword. These were the doors to what had once been Ghaleon's home here on Thaer. She had been visited previously with visions of his ghost walking these halls and sometimes given glimpses of past occurrences in her visions that would strike unannounced. Her nature of being a seer did not conventionally give her the ability to see any of the past, but she thought that there might be some magic embedded into this place that wanted her to see it for what it really was. Or maybe Ghaleon himself had sent her the visions so that she could better understand her duties in this life. Either way, she was thankful for what she knew and would do her best to use her knowledge for the greater good.

Anik was back at the Saliek camp studying and training under the tutelage of Regithal with some help from Zhannah. Regithal was grooming Anik to become the next Saliek'an since he knew that however long-lived he may be, there would someday be an end to his reign as Saliek'an. Either by death or by relinquishing it to someone better suited. Regithal preferred to have a well-trained successor in case the worst happened, and Anik was the best-suited candidate in his mind. Anik's leg had been better patched up by more skilled healers, but he still used the knobby stick that Kylie had given him on the mountain. He claimed that having a walking stick was fitting for an elementalist's image, but Scilla wondered if there was some lasting damage to his leg that pained him. Maybe the stick was helping him to walk better.

The Ignet had returned to Mahashta. Elasche was excelling at her training as an Ignet, gaining more tattoos from the portal trials steadily. Her training outside the portals now included staff fighting classes from Denna and archery classes with Lancet as opposed to just Dainn training her in all ways. Dainn and Lancet were friends again, and Denna and Lancet promised themselves to each other despite their now vast age difference. Grymm and Rosco had presented themselves to the royal family and had been given stations in the castle to protect the king and queen themselves. Though they were not the sole protectors of them, as Dainn had originally been to Elasche, this was an extremely high honor that they had been granted as Ignet. Beyond their normal duties, all of the Ignet spent time each day studying the portals and histories related to them. They took the elders' conversation seriously about keeping any splicers inside the portals and looking for other stranded Ignet to save.

Kylie and Mory were back in Arbore. They were working out something where they could be traveling emissaries for the court together since neither of them enjoyed being cooped up in the castle. The best way for them to battle the splicers was to teach people to be kind to one another so that evil could not grow inside them to nourish any growing splicers into existence. The best way for them to teach people to be kind was to lead by example and be openly kind to others across Krael and other planets. This was their rationale, and no one could refute it. And so, Kylie and Mory would travel the worlds together. Fueled by the happiness generated by their love for each other, they would rain kindness and joy upon all they met to make life a better existence for all. If they had to, they could fight a growing splicer, but to truly conquer all evil, they must appeal to the goodness within the hearts of all, or else no matter how many splicers they would slay, more would be born, and evil would never truly be purged from life.

***

Ghaleon smiled proudly down on Mory and Kylie. They had seen in mortality what Ghaleon had not. Evil could not be vanquished purely by slaying others who are perceived as evil. It had to be purged through goodness and positivity. Love, kindness, joy, happiness, understanding, and any other positive interactions had with people or creatures is what truly could rid the universe of evil.

Sonu stood by Ghaleon's side as they watched glimpses of the current happenings of the world. Ghaleon, remembering the curse of constant pain that he had laid upon Sonu's partial death, placed his hand on Sonu's back where his sword had punctured his body. With a deep breath, Ghaleon freed Sonu of the curse of pain that he himself had ashamedly burdened Sonu with.

Sonu cried out in bliss as he stretched his back in all directions, basking in his pain-free movement. Ghaleon smiled at the boy's ecstasy. "You are free, Sonu. Your debt is paid. You may cross into the realm of true death and peace if you desire."

"Thank you, kind sir, but no. I will remain in this partial death for a little while longer to see if there is anything else that I can do to help mortals while evil is still rampant."

Ghaleon nodded and smiled, turning his eyes back toward the worlds below. There were beautiful sunrises, peaceful sunsets, refreshing sprays of water near waterfalls, festive fields of flowers for frolicking, lovers looking into each other's eyes, friends adventuring together, bountiful feasts of delicious delicacies, and vast amounts of other things that could bring smiles to the faces of the living. So many magical moments that could be made, if only people took the time to watch, listen, and smell the sweet roses.

About the Author

Aerospace Engineer by day, fantasy author by night, Theresa Biehle has never let increasing age or responsibility dampen the wilds of her imagination or prevent her from following her dreams. She grew up in the small town of Ida, Michigan playing backyard baseball, reading fantasy novels, taking juicy bites out of garden-fresh tomatoes after splashing through muddy creeks, and sneaking through cornfields to make wishes on magic trees before obtaining her Bachelor's Degree in Aerospace Engineering and a Master's Degree in Space Systems Engineering from the University of Michigan. Job availability herded her into Leesburg, Virginia where she resides now. Softball equipment now sits in her basement, fantasy novels cover her bookshelves, tomatoes grow in her garden, and she has never stopped believing in the power of wishes and dreams.

Social

Follow me here for information on future writing endeavors, or support me with a book rating/review!

Facebook: biehletheresa
Instagram: theresabiehle
Goodreads Author: Theresa Biehle
Website: **www.theresabiehle.com**

Newsletter signup and bookshop are available on my website.

www.ingramcontent.com/pod-product-compliance
Lightning Source LLC
Chambersburg PA
CBHW020550310726
48979CB00008B/1159/J

9798985738827